CW00868449

YOU CANT HAVE YOUR YOUR CAKE AND EAT IT

A novel by

Kieron Blake

Boudoir Press.
http://boudoirpress.com

THE BLACK LEAF PUBLISHING GROUP
83 Clipstone Rd West
Forest Town, Mansfield
NG190ED
Nottinghamshire,
England

Acknowledgements

First and foremost, I would like to thank God for giving me the strength and fortitude it took to complete this project. When my to-do list piled up higher and higher and there was no end in sight, he was the one who helped me through all of the stressful times.

I want to thank Jean Charity and the rest of the team at Black Leaf Publishing for giving me the opportunity to write this book and allowing me the creative freedom to do it my way. I would also like to thank Stephen Jaspaul for having the patience and motivation to go through my work brutally and honestly, as well as performing a thorough edit of this book. It is much appreciated. A special thanks goes out to Sarah Wilson for constantly pushing, challenging and believing in me when the chips were down. Love you endlessly baby.

Personally speaking, I would like to thank the Brotherhood, NGC and the NW man dem for helping me along the path that has led me to this high point in my career. You guys have been great spiritual and professional mentors as well as great friends. Along with that, I have some amazing family who have been there from the start of my life. That being the case, I would like to extend a very special thank you to Auntie Rosie, Auntie Lillieth, Uncle Tony and Grandma Sadie. I couldn't have done it without you guys behind me.

Mostly, however, I want to thank my loving parents, Heather Blake and Albert Earle. Dad, even though you recently laid hands on a computer, your constant support and showing me the importance of networking makes me more driven to than to hear you say that you are proud of me. Mum, you brought me into the world and showed me the importance of knowing how to read and write (via Thomas the tank engine) and have an education, is my true driving force. The passion you showed for making sure that I became the intelligent and educated young man that I am today led to be so passionate in what I do. This book is every bit as much your accomplishment as it is mine.

Chapter One: Early Years, Michael

I never considered myself a 'battyman', a 'chi chi' man, a 'faggot', 'fudgepacker' or any other 'fuckeries' that society directed at homosexual people. I considered myself a young black heterosexual male, who had discreet homosexual tendencies. I felt like the guy from the film 'American Beauty' who was a closet gay, but was repulsed by gay activity. He was also a killer. I wasn't a killer. I had held a gun and a knife before, but never felt the desire to take someone's life.

The other concept applicable to me was that I was bisexual. "Bisexual people are greedy", my cousin said to me once. Maybe so, but I viewed my situation as a case that I wanted to have my cake and eat it. I also wanted to have a bit of 'Apple pie' and a bit of 'fudge'.

I went to a mixed primary school, where I proceeded to do a 'ting' with numerous girls. It was a case of playing 'kiss-chase' or 'you show me your fanny, and I will show you my Willy'. To say I had a homosexual experience at school is a bit dubious. I say dubious, because I couldn't see the homosexual connotations then, but if I was to look back at it now, it could have been considered a tad gay.

I remember a group of guys in my class, who used to go around spanking people's bottoms with their fingers. A tad freaky, I say, but I just didn't like it. I didn't like it because it stung. Also, I didn't because it wasn't right for young boys to be doing that (that's my straight, masculine side kicking it). However, I grew close with one of the guys. We had held hands at times, for example in assembly, but never in the playground. Perhaps this could be looked upon as male camaraderie in a homosexual way. This may be a harsh to look upon the friendship in that way. We were only kids, that

1

were innocent and pure, who didn't know any better, or did we?! Kids are curious at that age, and don't know any better. You are learning new stuff about yourself, your peers, and more importantly learning how to deal with it.

I grew up on watching Children BBC every weekday, viewing programmes such as SuperTed or watching Andy Peters host programmes. I remember when I was a child that Spotty, Superted's sidekick acted a bit 'funny' say to speak. He had a lisp, acted clumsy, spoke with a high pitched voice and acted very camp. I thought to myself "Nah man, that Spotty is a funny man". Wouldn't Spotty turn out to be a gay icon for the 80s. It seems like that a lot of the kid's programmes these days have a gay character. For example, look at Teletubbies. No one can't tell me that 'Tinky Winky' is not meant to be a 'battyman'. He's purple, wears a triangle on his head, and carries a handbag. If he is not supposed to be gay, then pigs can fly. Conversely, I know 'Dipsy' is meant to black. He can 'boggle', and wears a Jamiroquai hat. Is it really necessary for these programmes to show kids about gay people at that age? I am for educating the youth of today, but isn't up to children's parents to educate about them about gay people? However, there are some very narrow minded, confused people like myself that would give their kids ignorant knowledge. Maybe it is good that programmes like Teletubbies educate kids about gay people, as it is something awkward that parents have to endure. Could you imagine it, a child asking their mum, "Mummy, do gay people bum each other?"

Another kid's programme that has a gay character is Tom from 'Tots TV'. The character is just like Spotty. He acts clumsy, speaks with a lisp, clumsy, and speaks with a high pitched voice. It's this sort behaviour by gay men that I can't stand. This makes me think I am not a 'battyman', because I don't act like that. But who is say to that all gay men act like that? There are many straight acting gay men and they get by in society without people questioning their sexuality.

Let me come to Andy Peters. Don't get me wrong, I respect Andy Peters. He was one of the few 'brothers' to get a chance on T.V just like Trevor McDonald. Andy Peters held it up as he is still doing work for the BBC such as Top of the Pops. However I couldn't get over the way he spoke. The camp behaviour and the bizarre tank tops he used to wear really jarred me. To me, as a young child, it wasn't right that he was gay, and it was definitely not right that he was black and gay. But who I was to judge, as my later experiences would reflect. Each to their own I suppose.

When I was a kid growing up, I didn't really know any Black gay men apart from Andy Peters and Justin Fashanu. Justin Fashanu is another black gay man I respected. I respected him because he came out in the game of football, where there are no prisoners. Any gay man who could deal with homophobic chants and behaviour from fans on the terrace, players and even your own manager, was a man I could take my hat off too. I remember reading that when Justin Fashanu was having his problems, Nigel Clough labelled him a 'poofter out on the town". However, the pressures of being a young black gay footballer in the mainstream proved too much for poor Justin Fashanu. In 1997, he killed himself, R.I.P.

Television played a role in me 'finding' myself when I was younger. Everybody remembers the infamous lesbian kiss on Brookside. As a child, it got me going, and my erection was a reflection of that. However, it was another programme that really caught my attention. I remember it clearly. I was watching the television in my room before I went bed. I changed the channel to BBC 2. A drama series about young lawyers in London called 'This Life' was on. The opening scene of this episode had two guys making out in the shower. It was pretty explosive, erotic stuff to be shown after the watershed. It got me really excited and I proceeded to 'bash my bishop'. I didn't feel dirty, I just went with the flow.

As my primary school days drew to an end, I hoped that all of this was a phase. However, as I proceeded to go to secondary school, this 'phase' would rear its ugly head again...

Chapter 2 – Wonder years- Michael

I remember the drama about what high school my parents wanted to send me to. My parents wanted to send me to a private school. I was against this for two reasons. Firstly, I thought it was too much money for my parents to chalk up. More importantly, I was scared that I would turn into a 'battyman' if I went to a boy's boarding school. The thought of having to play 'soggy biscuit' or having a teacher or another student 'bugger' me was not the shout for me. If I had gone to a boarding school and turned gay, my father would have disowned me. He would have disowned me the same way the Pakistani father did to his son in the film, 'East is east'. However, you don't have to go to a same sex school to turn gay as I would find out.

I went to another mixed school. However I didn't get much 'love' from the chicks and I often found girls telling me their problems with their boyfriends. Perhaps I was a good listener or I was illustrating a queer quality where the gay man had his 'girlfriends' to bitch to him.

I remember there was two battymen at my school. They had their differences in terms of personalities, but they were both fundamentally gay. The first one was David. He was a very tall, skinny white guy. He had tried very hard to fight his gay side as he used to go out with enough girls. However I think he got to the point where he couldn't live a lie anymore, and decide to come out. I genuinely rate men who come out as gay. It must be very hard to do so. The fear of rejection and to be outcast by friends, family and having to make 'changes' to your lifestyle. He had done at a time when school kids can be very cruel. I remember when guys used to tease him for being gay and call him a 'battyman'. I thought it was 'dread' but I never stepped in and said 'allow him', in fear of my bredrins

5

calling me a 'battyman supporter' or getting rushed. Gay bashing was not popular as it used to be. I never forgot the time Robert Mugabe's henchmen decimated Peter Thatchell. Why a gay political activist would try and citizen's arrest a political tyrant, who detested gay people, was beyond me.

Then there was Brian. Another 'black battyman'. Maybe it was me, but I just couldn't stand the thought of black gay men, even if I had tendencies as one! It was just plain wrong. Black men had gone through enough? I mean slavery, civil rights and now gay pride. What the fuck?! It is just so taboo to be Black and 'batty'. The subject rarely gets discussed. I remember Brain had come out from the time I knew who he was. You could tell he was gay. Again just like David, he was skinny, camp, spoke with a high pitch voice like Mike Tyson and was feminine. He loved to do karaoke with the girls at school. I laughed so hard when I saw him performing. He was a 'batty man' that was out of tune and out of sync. Brian had two illicit affairs with guys from guys from school. He had an affair with one guy who got bullied so much he had to leave our school. This gay guy got bullied because he did stupid stuff and a lot of the time it was 'batty'. The other guy who Brian done a 'ting' with was apparently a straight guy in a loving relationship with a child present as well. I can't really say anything because I too was to do something very similar like that, and it would be a case of 'people who live in glass houses shouldn't throw stones'.

A poignant memory I had growing up as a confused teenage was taking home a gay magazine from the chill out room at college. I made sure that no one was watching me pull this stunt off. There had been a lot of uproar over this magazine. I knew whose it was, and me being curious, I took the magazine home. Some of the images turned me on and threw me into throws of ecstasy. I enjoyed the orgasm that I had from wanking upon seeing these images. However there was a difference this time from before. I felt dirty. I knew it was wrong and I would most probably go 'Hell' for it. But obviously it was the 'Devil' making me do all of this nasty stuff. I came from a Christian background, and the stuff I was doing was deplorable in the Bible. It was at this point I turned to this Holy Book and read how the Gays in Sodom and Gomorrah got burnt for their unholy actions. Let's not lie about it, the society we live in, is a modern day Sodom and Gomorrah. Gays marrying each other and having the access to raise kids is downright wrong. Gays in the Church is wrong. The whole of the 'Battyman movement' is wrong, and here was me in the middle, not sure which team to 'bat' for. This whole episode made me sick and upset, so much that I cried myself to sleep...

I did my A levels in college and did well. However I wasn't ready to go to uni. I wanted to travel before I went uni, and it was this travelling that opened my eyes more...

Chapter 3 –Globetrotter- Michael

I took a gay year; sorry I mean a gap year after my A' levels. I saved enough money from my part time telesales job along with the commission and overtime to go travelling for 6 months. But the question was where would I go? Caribbean? I had been to Jamaica, Barbados and Trinidad so many times and the other small islands didn't appeal to me. What about the Americas. North America was just Canada and the USA, and I could go there anytime. The only place in South America that remotely appealed to me was Brazil. Rio de Janeiro, Cape of God, Brazilian chicks, Samba carnival, football, beaches, by Jobe that would have been the one for me. However I didn't feel ready for Brazil. Why? Because I didn't want to be so far away from home, and what if I was kidnapped and taken to the Amazon Forest as a hostage. Who would rescue me? Who would pay my ransom money? Anyone that has seen the film 'City of God' knows Brazil can be pretty 'gully and grimy'.

I picked up my map of the world and thought, why don't I use my constitutional right of being a European citizen and travel around Europe. It was close to home and there would be so much to do or would there?

The term 'Black European' to me does not exist. Whenever I filled out a diversity form, I always saw 'Black Caribbean', 'Black African', 'Black Other', but never 'Black European'. The term Black Gay European does not exist. Europeans do not how to deal with Black people and more to the point Black gay men. Tell a lie, they can handle a gay Black man. This is because a gay Black man is less of a threat to them. Europeans do not how to deal with Black people due to tradition and history, a MEP once told me. The amount of times on my travel of Europe I had people assume I was 'African' and I shocked them when I spoke such good English was unaccountable. 'How long you been in England?' a dumb ignorant Parisian had said to me in a bar in Paris. "My entire life dude", I replied. I could see the perplexity in his face. I even whipped out my British passport to prove my point, and he was still baffled. The intricacies of being Black British confused him immensely. To him and other Europeans, Black Europeans didn't exist. They were all Africans who were immigrants who worked in low paid jobs such as cleaners and security, and had big bums and big dicks. Even if a Black European was working in a well-respected job, it was frowned upon by their White European counterparts, by a notion of 'you're not supposed to be here'.

The icing on the cake came in this conversation with this Parisian pig. He asked me what team do Black people support in England. I looked at him in such dismay and left the bar without finishing my drink to cries of "per quoi? What did I say, what did I do?" This was the 21st century and Black people still had to deal with this shit. I swear slavery ended years ago?!

You might have guessed it. France was the first stop on my tour of Europe. I went to Paris, Versailles, Boulogne, Calais, Marseille, Lyon and Toulouse. I also went Monaco and St Tropez, living it up with the rich and famous. It was amazing to see how the other half lived but it sure wasn't my cup of tea. It was in France that I encountered a most bizarre sexual experience. As I left that bar, I bumped into this Black Canadian women that I had seen on my travels. We went for a drink and then for a 'nightcap' at hers. No sooner had we got in, we were ripping each other's clothes off. I was sucking her beautiful, big Nubian breasts as she wanked my throbbing shaft. I touched her pussy and it was wetter than the Niagara Falls. At this point, she told me to stop. She proceeded to get on all fours and pointed to me to put my dick into her wet pussy. I was so horny, I didn't even 'strap up'. I just rammed my dick in her and proceeded to doggy her senseless, grabbing her hair as she moaned and groaned. I was on the verge of climax, when she pulled away, turned around to face me, grabbed my dick, so that I could cum on her breasts. I did so and it felt great but grimy. It felt like I was in a porno. It was at this point, things got grimier and a bit gritty. Jackie that was her name totally flipped the script. "Your man enough to cum on my breast. Now be man enough to lick your cum of my breasts!" I looked at her with such dismay and confusion. She wanted me to lick my own cum off her breasts. She was either too freaky or thought I was some battyman?! Whatever the deal, I grabbed my clothes and darted towards the door. In the background I could her saying "Don't go, I was only joking!" I never saw Jackie again. That encounter still sends a shiver down my spine...

I left France to go Spain and Portugal. Enjoying the sun, sea and the sights. My day consisted of drinking sangria, fucking 'broads' and sleeping in the sun. What more could a man what in life? But this was the thing I wanted more. The whole point of me travelling was to find myself, and that I hadn't done that yet. I went to Germany for a couple of days, and only to be hounded out of Berlin by a bunch of neo Nazis who thought I was trying to attack an old granny. I was actually trying to help when she fell. So much for being the 'good old Black Samaritan'!

I went back to the hostel. I sat on my bed, disillusioned with my travelling so far. There had been good times but I felt the bad times were starting to outweigh the good. I wanted to go home. I missed England, my family, my friends and home comforts. However, something in the back of my head said to me that I hadn't completed what I set out to do. The thing in my head knew what it was, and deep down I knew what it was. It was my need to find my sexuality, without anyone or anything influencing my decision on the matter. I went to sleep happy knowing what I needed to do.

I woke up. It was after one in the afternoon. I realised my funds were soon drying up, and if I wanted to put my plans into fruition say to speak, I would need to make my moves fast. But one thing bugged me. Where would I go? Not knowing where to go. I started to throw my tennis ball against the wall to get inspiration. I did this when I didn't have any ideas on a particular subject. Then it came to me. I would go to Holland. I would go to the red light district of Amsterdam...

Chapter 4 Amsterdam-Michael

I got to Amsterdam the next day, and immediately checked into another hostel. After dropping off my luggage, I took a walk through Amsterdam. It was so relaxed, so 'laizzez faire'. I proceeded to make my way to the red light district. I went to a coffee shop where I 'coched' and had a nice 'zoot'. I 'monged' out in the café and fell asleep. When I awoke, it was late afternoon. I was feeling horny and randy, so I decide to visit a sex shop. I went upstairs to find that they had booths that you could watch porn in. I put about 20 Euros in the booth and proceeded to watch porn. There were 150 channels of illicit stuff. Everything was on these channels. Black on Black sex, White on White sex, Animal sex (I remember particularly a dog fucking a woman doggy style, that's fucked up!), over 50's /60's sex (Grannies being fucked by young stallions), bondage/Dominatrix and gay sex. I whipped out my dick and proceeded to bash off. I buss all over my thigh, and used the tissue in the booth to clean up. This time, I didn't feel guilty. Maybe this was because I was still charged from the weed that I had taken big boy 'tokes' on. My inhibitions had gone. Maybe I thought I didn't give a fuck and there was no one here to tell me nothing. I left the shop to go to the red light district to look at the 'hoes' in the window, scantily dressed in their bras and thongs. They all had the same aim. Their aim was to entice punters to having sex with them, and get their day's earnings.

I woke up and it was 10pm. I had somehow made my way back to the hostel in one piece and 'K'Od' on the bed. I decided that I wanted to enjoy the nightlife. I still had some weed, so before I had a shower, I smoked a big fat spliff to myself. Feeling really mellow, I had a hot shower, got dressed and hit the town. I decided that I would venture to a gay bar. Surely there would be some in Amsterdam. I never had been to a gay bar before, or on this trip of sexual exploration. I thought I had nothing to lose. You can always tell a gay bar. It has a distinctive flag with multi colours on it. I thought fuck it. I walked into the bar and there were more men than I expected. There were a few women, but the ratio was 5 men to 1 girl. I could see and feel the looks, as me, Michael Brown, this well-built Black guy walked up to this bar, this gay bar. Some guys were looking at me, as if to say to say "Yeah, I want a piece of you". There were guys who were in awe of me and didn't know what to think of me. Then you had the 'rude boys' who were screwing me because I was on their 'territory'. I couldn't give two fucks. I ordered a large rum and coke and made my way to a quiet spot. I would take the evening in by watching how these gays would interact and gyrate with each other. As I listened to the funky house music blaring loud, this white guy approached me, and asked if I minded him joining me at my table. I was cool. We started to talk. He was ok. Tall, skinny, dark hair guy was from England too. Working for a sales company in Amsterdam, his name was Jared. As the drinks poured in, we continued to talk about each other's lifestyles, what we wanted, what we liked and how we were going to get it. Then the inevitable happened. "Do you want to come back to mine and chill?" asked Jared. Back in the day, I would have said no, and the hesitance was present on my countenance, but I thought 'fuck it'. I'm away, just go with the flow.

We got a cab back to Jared's. His place was nice. You could tell that this job paid well. Plasma T.V, Sony Vaio laptop and Ikea furniture. The list could go on. We sat on his sofa, drinking the wine, which seemed to be just flowing. At this time, we were both tipsy, whereas Jared was very 'touchy feely'. Then Jared just dropped it so raw. "Are you gay?" From this point onwards, I don't remember anything else.

I started to come around from the weed to find a sharp pain in my backside. I was on my stomach. That t was strange. I'm sure I was asleep on my back. I could hear grunting. I looked over my shoulder. That 'bastard' Jared was raping me as I slept. I screamed "Get the fuck of me". I turned over and punched him in his face. He fell off me. Jared had previously asked me if I was 'gay'. The answer now was "Hell No!" My backside was stinging at that point. I could feel tricklets of blood running down my leg. I looked at Jared. He was naked but there was no condom on his dick. Where was it?! Had it fallen off when I fought him off me? Maybe he hadn't? I went for the latter, fuelled by the view that he might have infected me with something. If that was the arse, it was 'curtains for me'. Jared was recovering. "Chill Michael", he said calmly. He had obviously done this before. Before he could speak, I punched him clean in his mouth, and started to throttle him. My straight heterosexual macho self was coming out as I choked the fucker who raped me! I screamed "You raped me! You violated me while I slept!" Jared couldn't answer me. He was choking and turning red. My rational side kicked in. I relinquished my grip of his neck. I was so angry. I was fuming that I could have been so stupid to go back with a complete stranger that I didn't know. This is why I don't do one night stands. I put on my clothes with such urgency. Jared came up. Still recovering, he said, "You won't tell anyone? My career will be in ruins". I looked at him. "I'm gonna tell the Police and anyone who will believe me!" Jared panicked. "Don't tell the Police. I got lots of money; you can have all of it!" I didn't want this rapist money. However, I knew people in institutions are the most prejudiced people in the world. Power gets to them. They wouldn't believe me. It would be my word against his. They would be like, "dumb black nigger, got what he deserved". My pride kicked in. I sold myself short. "Give me all the money that you got on your now. I want all your credit cards and their pins", I protested. I was a typical

14

'nigga', hustling for that pea. Jared got his wallet. "Take them all. The pins are 1980 for all of them". I took the money and the credit cards. I looked at Jared with disgust. "You dirty faggot!" I shouted at him. Jared couldn't look at me. As I left, I kicked him and spat on him. Just like he had degraded me, I would degrade him. That was my 'gay bashing' for the day.

I got a cab back to the town centre. I had already had 2000 Euros from Jared's wallet, but I wanted more 'compensation', for what that bastard did to me. I wanted reparations for the emotional and physical trauma he had given me. Jared had given me 2 credit cards, and a debit card. Going to different cash machines in Amsterdam, I withdrew all that I could from all the three cards. It was long going to the shops and buying stuff with these cards, and 'baiting' up my Black face. I threatened Jared before I left. I said if he told anyone about the cards, I would come and expose him for the rapist that he was, and I would kill him. By the time I had finished, I nearly had 8 grand in Euros.

I made my way back to the hostel. I went straight into the shower, and shut the door. I turned the shower to full blast. I proceeded to wash myself excessively. I felt dirty, used and violated. I wanted to wash that 'man' off me and was away my sin. I was asking for trouble doing what I did. I needed to also accept some responsibility for what had happened. Regardless, I broke down and cried violently. I felt like Luke from 'Hollyoaks' after he got raped. Why me?! What did I do to deserve this? The difference in the rapes that happened to me and Luke was he was conscious when he got raped. There was me thinking that male rape didn't happened. It did and I was sentiment to it. I hated gay people now and I hated Europe. My experience in Europe was tainted by racists, freaks, rapists and fucking 'poofters'. I wasn't gay. I cried even more. I wanted to go home…

Chapter 5 Adulthood Michael

I came back to England a month early. With about 7 grand in Euros in toll, I went for a STD test straight away. The first two weeks back were harrowing, as I waited for my test results. They came back negative; I was a much relived man. I put the money from Amsterdam into a cash ISA, and left it there as a reminder of my foolishness abroad.

I started university in September. I went to Nottingham to study Law. First year of uni was a blast. Raving every week, getting drunk every week. Meeting new chicks, and banging them. I was fresh from LDN. It was my time. The first year didn't count, just between missing lectures. I was constantly blazing, playing Mario kart on the N64, and watching Countdown. My stable diet consisted of Snakebites and Baked Beans (with Black pepper and onion) on toast.

It was my first year that I set my eyes upon Michelle. She was beautiful, intelligent and more importantly a strong Black woman. I never thought in a million years that two years later I would be with her. I remember when I spoke to her, we just seemed to click. She was friends with a couple of chicks in my class. I wanted to make her my wifey from day 1 set eyes on her. However, I didn't want to be tied down so early on in my uni career. I wanted to have my wicked way with as many different types of women as I could possibly could before I settled down. I think Michelle detected this from me. "You love a girls company", she said to me once when I 'jammed' in her room. I replied, "Is that what you think?" Who would think that this was coming from a guy, who the other year was tethering to fudge rather than apple pie?! It was at that point I wanted to have Michelle and fuck her. However I didn't want to. It was more a case I respected her and I didn't want to her be one of my 'tings'. I knew she liked me and I liked her, but we remained friends. I passed my test with her on this occasion, just like I passed the first year.

Second year was a totally different ball game. Second year counted. I reduced my blazing, although the Amsterdam Purple Haze came handy when I did all night sessions for essays. I often had mind blocks, and smoking that shit gave me some, mad, intelligent bursts where I would write some real deep shit. I was literally thinking outside the box. Playing Mario Kart on the N64 was replaced by Pro Evolution on Play station 2. My stable diet was now Red Bull and Ginsters pasties.

Second year was hard. I really worked hard to 'bust my balls' with my uni work. I dramatically cut down my drinking and raving. I was also lacking a bit of stability, and it was a good timing that I got with Michelle. Every now and then, I would remember what happened in Amsterdam, and it would depress me. One day, I would be up, other days I would be down. Michelle helped me by time. I remember there was a uni rave and I saw here there. A slow jam went on, and I made a b'line for her. I danced behind her. She acknowledged my presence. I pulled her in and held her tightly and gently. The dance seemed to last forever. After the rave, I saw her. She was 'jamming' with her 'bredrins'. I said to her if she wanted to come back to mine for a 'coffee'. She obliged. We got a cab back to mine. No sooner had we got in my room, it was on. I was kissing her neck and fingering her. She grabbed my throbbing dick and it pulled it up and down. I reached for her left breast and sucked on her nipple and she moaned gleefully. My fingers were still down her crutch, and it was wetter than the River Thames down there. I stopped fingering her. I whispered in her ear, "Are you ready?" She looked at me and nodded. She whispered back "Have you got any protection?" I was like "No". A bit perturbed by my response, she uttered "I'm on the pill". I said "Cool". I lay Michelle on the bed. I lay on top of her and placed my dick in her. She moaned as I entered her. I started to ride her, slowly but surely as 'Jodeci' played in the background. I didn't unleash my entire Arsenal because when I gave her leg, foot pon shoulder, Michelle couldn't take it. The joys of fucking Black women. Michelle proceeded to ride me. It was good. Her chocolate body was straddling me as I placed my hands over erected nipples. She looked at me straight in the eye and she moaned and groaned. She cried "Oh Michael!" It felt like the scene from 'Rolling with the Nines', where the mixed race girl was riding Val Blackwood. I could relate to Val, because right now everything was 'bless'. Michelle started to cum. The moaning and groaning got louder, as she violently shaked and rattled. She scratched my chest and belly as she climaxed. She had finished, but I was yet to come. Wiping the sweat from her brow, she asked if I wanted to doggy her. I obliged. I got her on all fours. I could see her wet pussy dripping. This turned me on. I pushed my dick in her. She moaned. I started to pound away at her swollen pussy as she moaned and called 'Michael'. You know it's a good doggy, when the chick looks back at you when you're dogging her, and this was what Michelle was doing. I stated to feel myself coming and I drew her in closer. I growled like a wolf when I came. We cuddled and I looked at her, she looked at me. The love was there from the beginning, and this was the start of our troubled relationship.

Throughout the second year, we would help each other out through the good and bad times. We would go around each other's places and help each other with our work. It was nice to know that the weekends, I could come home from work to find my dinner was cooked. We would enjoy lovely dinners, the watching of DVDs and the odd drinking and blazing sessions. Michelle didn't really drink and smoke and that bugged me. It bugged me because I felt she was too reserved and too prim and proper. I wanted her to loosen up but as our relationship progressed, I would find that I couldn't force that on her. If Michelle wanted to do that, she would have to do that herself.

Third year was really hard. I was still with Michelle, and that was what helped me get through third year. When the chips were down, I would think about the rape. It still bugged me. I thought about seeing a Counsellor to get over it, but something inside of me told I didn't need one. I knew that I couldn't be down all the time. I put myself out 110% and that was reflected in my dissertation. There was no raving and no drinking. This was replaced with me in my head down in the books. Blazing didn't exist to me anymore. Michelle hated the fact that I blazed. I blazed as it helped me escape short term from my problems, but as Michelle would always point out that my problems would still be there. "It's a nasty habit", she would protest vehemently. I knew she was glad that I stopped blazing in the final year. I still played Pro Evolution 4 with the 'man dem' but that was every now and then. I was always at a p.c or laptop. Being with Michelle and being on proper lock down worked because we both came out with 2.1's...

Chapter 6 Michelle

I have been with Michael for 3 years now, but I don't think he is the one for me. I would have thought that now we're back in London, things would have changed, but they haven't. They have got worse. We argue constantly. I'm not sure if I'm in love with him anymore. I know he is sweet and caring, but he irritates me all the fucking time. He lets others decide his fate for him. What the fuck?! He supposed to be a man, not a boy. He supposed to take charge of situations. I know he isn't earning much or any money at the moment, but it would be nice if he could pay for me at dinner instead of going halves all the time. He should be taking me out shopping. Fuck it, I got my own money. He's in his early twenties and he doesn't drive. That's loose. Can't he see I'm not happy anymore? He bought me a chain when we first started dating. I don't wear it anymore. I wear the chain that a real man bought me. My Dad bought that chain for me. Why can't he be like my Dad? A strong powerful Black man is what I want. I know it burns him that I don't wear the chain that he bought me, but he needs to fix up. All he does is smoke weed, play Playstation and make tunes with Jason. That's something a 'wasteman' does. Michael is lucky to be with me and he needs to recognize that. I am too good for him. Who was there when he was going through his problems at uni? Me! He's too up and down for me. I'm sure he's suffering from depression. He needs to stop blazing and go see a shrink. I'm not even attracted to him anymore. He looks rough all the time. Going barbers once a month. He should be going twice a month like other Black guys. I can't take the beard and his picky hair. It doesn't reflect his beauty. He always says he's ugly. When I ask him why he says that, he tells me his Mum told him that. I got issues with his Mum, but truth be told that I don't say anything to him or her about it. I've gone off sex with Michael too. I don't like kissing, but he insists on doing it. I know he is

20

a stocky guy, but he has let himself go. I'm sure he's getting a beer belly. I don't like when Michael rides me. He's too big for me in his size and his dick. I only like doggy and when I ride him. I just prefer it when he licks me out and I wank him. I love when he licks me out.

Michael is shit with money. It really pisses me off because of that. I don't know why I haven't finished it with him. I think he would switch if I dumped him. I think he would be in a state, where he might even kill himself. I just think it would be callous of me to do that to him as he's such a nice guy, but maybe it's the best for him...

The other night when Michael was out, my friend Ola came round to see me. We have been friends for years. I know he fancies me. Anyway, I told him my situation. He said "leave him and be with me". I looked at Ola with bewilderment. I couldn't believe what I heard. I was numb and shocked. At this point Ola put his arm around me and kissed me. Maybe it was the wine and I was feeling tipsy, but I kissed him back. Ola whispered in my ear, "I've been waiting for years to do that to you". I looked back at him gleefully. I know it would burn Michael if I left him for Ola. This is because Michael always felt Ola had fancied me for time, and because Ola is African, Nigerian to be precise. "Do you still hear from that Boob- boo?" Michael would say to me. Conversely Ola, would ask me "Has that waste Jamo got a job yet?" West Indian guys can't stand when West Indians girls go out with African guys. African guys treat their women better, are educated and more financially stable. Most West Indians guys are 'wastemen'. If they're not 'blazing' weed, then they are 'shotting' it. If they haven't got a job, then they're making beats on the Playstation and eating fried chicken from the chicken shop. At the start of this relationship, Michael didn't fit that criteria at all, but now he was fitting it quite well. Sod it, he needs to fix up. As these thoughts crossed my mind, I felt Ola's hand touching my wet pussy. Suddenly I heard the key turning in the front door...

Chapter 7 Michael

It was 7.30 am when I looked at the clock on my bedside table. Michelle was on the other side of the bed. She had been distant throughout the night. When I asked if she wanted a cuddle, she fiercely declined. When I tried to cuddle her in the night, she just pushed me away. Maybe something was on her mind, or maybe it was plain PMT. Feeling randy, I grinded myself on the back of her and kissed her neck. It felt like she was rolling her eyes. "Do you want me to lick you out?" I asked. "No" was the answer I got for my troubles. I didn't like being rejected. Feeling frustrated, I blurted out "I'm horny and I want to fuck you!" Michelle looked at me with shock. She didn't say anything. She peeled off her knickers and placed my hand on her pussy. Using my fingers, she rubbed them against her clitoris. She started to moan. I wasn't feeling it at all. The sex had become monotonous, repetitive and a tad boring. I knew the sequence of events. I would rub or lick her clit. She would orgasm and cum. I would then either fuck her doggy or missionary. I would 'buss my nut'. We would share a fake kiss, cuddle and then fall asleep. It wasn't making love. It was actually boring fucking. The sequence kicked in, and when I was riding her, I didn't even look at Michelle. I kept my head over her left shoulder. Michelle didn't like to kiss during sex. She felt distracted when we did it. Kissing was always a yes for me. I loved it as t heightened the passion during love making sessions. I just wanted to hurry up and cum. This sex was pointless. This sex was rubbish. Serve me right for wanting/demanding sex. I came in Michelle and didn't make a noise. I removed myself from Michelle's vagina.

"Did you cum?"

"Yeah",

I replied seemingly not bothered when really I was. I rolled over and went back to sleep.

I woke again. This time was it was 9.37 am. Michelle was gone. She had gone to work. I checked my phone. I had a voicemail. I picked up my Nokia 6310, the best phone ever. I listened to the message. It was Claire, the lady from the temping agency. She told me she had a job that I might be interested and if I wanted it, I should come to the office this morning. I rang Claire back and confirmed I would be coming through to discuss the job. I came off the phone. I didn't need to watch any porn as I had already released my load. I went to the bathroom and had a shower.

The time was now 10.15 am. I left the flat and walked to the bus stop to go to Central. Something told me that something was going to come good out of this morning. I jumped onto the bus and proceeded to go upstairs. As I reached the top deck, I noticed it was quite empty, but this didn't deter me from seeing this white girl that I had seen a lot on this bus. She was a brunette with blonde highlights. She had a nice smile and big buxom breasts. She also had a fat ass to match as well. She was the voluptuous girl that I, Michael Brown would normally go for. Two problems sprung to my mind. Firstly I was seeing Michelle and secondly, this girl was white. However, my relationship was a sham at the moment, so I had nothing to lose. Moreover, the fact that she was white bugged me. A white woman was the reason that I got an STI when I was younger. A white woman was the reason my cousin was in HMP, when she cried 'wolf'. A white woman was the reason that my best friend got into so much trouble. Did I want to endure all of the above? Did I want to have an inter-racial relationship with this girl and end up having mixed race kids known as 'Ashley', 'Dale' and 'Jade'? These were the names of mix race people I knew. Did I want to have kids who thought they had the best of both world or if they were asked what colour they were, they could possibly come out with the answer 'Brown'? Fuck that. However, white women did have their pros as well. I always saw white women as dirty and loose. Give them a couple of drinks, their tits and fanny would be all yours. This is why I frequented clubs in Watford and Romford. Black men were like dynamite in those places. However, I was a hypocrite as well. I didn't like in particular seeing Black footballers and Black sporting figures with white women. Why they couldn't find a decent Nubian princess, I always asked myself. My friends would always say it was because of their environment. These Black footballers would frequently visit clubs that were for celebrities and rich people. In these places, there were more likely to be loads of white women as opposed to the fraction of Black women there. It should be also noted that these clubs have been known to turn away Black women, as they are supposed to attract gangster wannabees. Furthermore, these white women were attracted to these players wealth and would be quick to 'rape' them of their acquired wealth should they get married and then divorced. Frank Bruno was a casualty of this. Moreover, Frank Bruno came running back to Black people when his 'beloved' Laura left him when he went 'cuckoo'. Black footballers such as Ian Wright (although he did catch a case of 'Jungle Fever) and Andy Cole earned my respect as they had Black wives.

The white woman, who gave me a STI, was filthy and was up for some 'grimy shit'. I remember hitting her in the forehead with my dick. I refer to this degrading yet satisfying act as 'cockboxing'. White women loved having a big black dick in them, and white men hated that. Asian men were the same. They deplored their women being with Black men. Black men, we were envy of all other men. My friend Jerome, had a white girl on lock down for time. He had been with her ages. He didn't have a job. He blazed all day. He made beats on Fruityloops all day. He drove her car, whilst she worked hard all day. As long as she had her trophy Black man, and a hard Black dick to come home at the end of the day, that was all she cared about. With all these thoughts running through my head, I would need to dispossess them if I wanted this girl's digits. I said to her "Excuse me, I have seen you on the bus all the time, and just wanted to say I think you are really pretty". I had game and had to say something that would make her feel sweet and be putty in my hands. The white girl smiled and blushed.

"What's your name?"

"Gemma, what's yours?"

"They call me Brown, Michael Brown",

The corniness of the quote similar to that used in James Bond films, made us laugh. We engaged in conversation. The thing that struck me the most was that she was a copper, a fed, Babylon, 5-0. At that point, I just thought about beating her pussy with my hard Black truncheon!

"Arrested a lot of people?"

"A few"

"You could arrest me any day of the week"

She laughed at me even more. I was intrigued by her and I could see she was intrigued by me too. We were similar in many ways. We both went university. She was doing a criminology degree, but she dropped out to become a police officer. She had her head screwed on. I liked that as most white girls I met were common and slags. The bus approached Brixton station, and I needed to get off.

"Can I have your number please?"

"I don't normally give out my number, but your different, I like you"

I smiled. I handed her my phone and she put her number into it. My ploy had worked. Job done. Mission complete. I wished her a good day and told her I would be in touch. She smiled. I got off the bus and walked into Brixton station. My day would get better. The temping agency managed to get me a temping job. I accepted it. I would start on Monday.

Chapter 8 Gemma

The bus had left Brixton station. I had just met a cool, pleasant Black guy called Michael. He was really nice. He made me laugh and smile. Not many could do that for me. I don't normally go for Black guys. Perhaps I was just generalizing or stereotyping them but I have had bad experiences with them. They all think the world owes them something. It must be a slavery thing, even though slavery ended many years ago. They need to get over it. I had arrested a few of them as a law enforcing officer. Most of them were either drug dealers or gun tooting gangsters. Whenever we would stop them, it would be the same boring repetitive answer; "Its cos I'm Black". That excuse was getting old and dated. 8 out of 10 times, we were stopping them for drug or gun offences. Conversely, Michael was not like other Black guys I had come across in my life. He wasn't rude or aggressive. He was calm, polite and well spoken. He must be African. He had many positive attributes. He had a degree in Law and wanted to do something with his life. A lot of Black guys that I had nicked were jobless, on the dole, uneducated and broke. I could tell Michael had money. He dressed nicely. His hair was short and neat. His beard was trimmed exceptionally well. No doubt he had a big dick as well. I knew Black guys were promiscuous. There's a Black guy that lives on my road. The amount of different women I see leaving his house amazes me. I know my father wouldn't approve of me dating a Black guy. He was mugged by a Black guy a few years ago, and that changed his perception of Black people. "Never liked them", Dad said one day. "Britain used to be great, but those monkeys came over back in the 60s ad took our jobs and our women! Now you got bloody refugees from Kosovo trying to take over. It's bloody disgusting". It made Dad sound bitter. He had become was even more bitter when Mum passed away a few years with breast cancer, but I still loved him anyway.

As the bus travelled over Vauxhall Bridge, I smiled and hoped Michael would call me...

Chapter 9, Michael New Job

It was Monday morning. It was the start of my new temping job. I had a good weekend. I went to the cinema and a restaurant with Michelle on Saturday. On Sunday, we chilled. We didn't argue the whole weekend. It made a change from the constant belittling I would receive from her. Maybe it was to do with the fact that I got this job. I was going to be working for Transport for London as a researcher. It was good money as well. I turned to my left and Michelle was asleep in my arms. She woke up.

"Morning Sweetie"

"Morning Babes"

"How are you feeling about your first day?"

"Nervous I guess"

"You will be ok, I'm so proud that you got a job. Maybe things will start going your way", Michelle gesticulated. With that she gave me a kiss and backed into me, pulling my arms around her waist as I held her tight. If there was one thing I knew, myself and Michelle both liked cuddling. It reflected the somewhat closeness that we seemed to have. We seemed to have cuddled for about 10 minutes, for which it seemed like an eternity.

"I have to get ready; I don't want to be late"

"Oh", I was really enjoying that"

"Don't worry you can have another one later"

I jumped into the shower, excited by the thought that I would be working, and money would be coming in again.

The time was now 8.45 am. I was waiting at the bus stop. My bus pulled up and I got on it. I felt so excited that I had a job, even if it was a temporary one. I could pay my bills, look after myself and treat Michelle for an occasional meal. I got up the stairs, and then it hit me. It was déjà vu again. Gemma, the white chick I 'chirpsed' on Friday was on the bus. She looked sexy just like before. Our eyes met, and we both smiled. I sat next to her, and apologised straight away for not being in contact with her. She was cool with it. It was like she knew the 'coo'. We started to talk, and it felt like we had known each other for a long time. I liked Gemma. I liked her because we had a lot of things in common. We both liked 'South Park'; both were Leos and similar family background and problems. She was totally different to Michelle. Randomly, I asked Gemma the infamous question.

"Would you like to go for a drink in the week?"

"Of course I would!"

"I will call you later and we'll arrange something"

She smiled. I could see my stop was coming. I got up and kissed her cheek. She smiled again. Gemma had a nice smile. We said 'bye' simultaneously. It was something out of a romantic movie. I got off the bus and proceeded to go into Brixton station.

I got to Kings Cross at 9.45 am. The place I was going to was around the back of the station. I found it with ease. I was to ask for Nathan when I got to the reception. I did so when I arrived, and was greeted by a short, skinny mix race guy. "You must be Michael?" he asked. "Yes", I replied. We shook hands, and proceeded to the main office. We got to the door, and Nathan stopped me. "Before we go in I want to ask you a question". I was like go for it. "Do you have a problem with me being gay?" he asked. I won't lie; I was taken aback by his question. "I don't have a problem with gays", I replied. What a lie I had just told! I had a lot of problems with gays. I wasn't sure if I was gay/bisexual, one of them raped me, and now I had one of them asking me if I had a problem with him being gay?! If I had my way I would have said I do have a big problem with gays or the 'battyman' movement. Regaining my composure, I retorted, "Why did you ask me that?" Nathan said he liked to be open about his sexuality from the start of any relationship he had with anyone. I sensed he and others couldn't deal with his sexuality, and people finding out him being gay. However it was cool with me for now. For the next couple of weeks, Nathan would shadow me as I temped at this place. He would show me the ropes, show me who he perceived was cool and not cool. By the end of my first week, I was confident in what I was doing and knew about all about the office politics...

Chapter 10 Nathan

Today, I met a real nice Black guy at work called Michael. He's really cool and easy to get along with. He must be the first Black guy that is genuinely at ease with me being gay. Black guys don't like the fact that I'm gay. It's not like I want to fuck them, although many of them are cute. It was always them who made noise about me being gay. "Bun that chi-chi man!" or 'fucking battyman' is what I have had to deal with from them. They must be the most homophobic people I have come across. I blame the dancehall stars for some of the animosity that gays like me have to deal with. Look at guys like 'Beenie man' (who I feel is a closet gay), 'Bounty Killer' and 'Buju Banton' promoting all that hatred for gays, it's wrong. Tunes like 'Bun off the Chi-Chi" are so wrong. You would have thought that these artists would have learned from 'Shabba Ranks' and his derogatory comments that he made on 'The Word'. His career was never the same after those comments. It nose- dived dramatically.

Black youths were always quick to say 'bun off the chi-chi man', but little did they realise that it was actually the 'chi- chi man who was bunning them'. I say this because a lot of gays are in the positions of power. There are many in the media. Channel 4 is an example of this. They are many in the police force and the Houses of Parliament. Black people never like the way they are construed in the media. Maybe if they were not so anti gay, they might be better represented rather than having Gus, a black lay about dustbin man on 'Eastenders' represent them. Black youths never thought that the same 'battyman' who they were obliterating, was the same 'battyman' implementing rules to increase more 'stop and search' on them. Black youths needed to stop being fickle and ignorant. They needed to 'wake up and smell the coffee'.

I remember one of my Black male clients 'dissed' me when one of our sessions didn't go to plan. "Look at you!" he said. "Your mix-race and you're a battyman! You must be so fucked up", he added. "So why you fucking me then?" I asked. I got slap in my face for my insolence. I suppose that's what happens when you rent out your batty. I don't regret it. I had bills to pay, and I was doing something that I enjoyed; being fucked.

Back to Michael, he didn't flinch when I told him I was gay. He just took it for what it was. I assumed he had 'relations' with gay people before, and this was why he was so calm and laidback about it all. He reminded me of my girlfriends. Speaking of my girlfriends, they were similar to Black youths. They weren't anti gay, but they were fickle and naive. They saw models and celebrities as role models. They always moaned that they could never find clothes to fit them. I always told it was because most fashion designers were gay men like Giovanni Versace. They could never see the logic or the reverse psychology of it all. Gay male fashion designers would make clothes designed for skinny woman. All women of all shapes and sizes would do anything to wear the latest designs. Most would become anorexic or bulimic in order to fit into these designs. Some would kill themselves in order to fit into designers. Also some of the designs were awful, but women would flock to buy them as they were on the catwalk. Ultimately, men would become less attracted to these women, and they would become vulnerable to homosexual guys like me who would convert them. I reckon I could convert Michael, so his girlfriend(s) better watch out. Heterosexual women couldn't see that fashion designed for them was a ploy by cunning and intelligent gay men. The fewer women or less attractive women out there meant more men for disposal by gay men. Call it a conspiracy, I called it gay domination and this was why I was proud to be gay.

Chapter 11 Michael, meeting Gemma

It was Friday, and my first week of work was passé. Some aspects of the job were boring. Other parts of the work were bearable. Nathan helped me a lot definitely. I didn't care that he was gay. He was a sound guy. Nathan and the others were going for drink after work, but I couldn't make it. I had other plans. I was meeting Gemma. I got round to texting her and arranged to meet up with her at Liverpool Street for a drink.

I had got out of work to find Michelle was calling me. I answered the phone. "Hello". She replied, "Hiya Babes". She seemed like she was in a good mood for once. She went on "What time you coming home, I thought we could go for a meal to celebrate your first week at your job". It was a sweet thing to ask, but to be honest I wasn't feeling it for two reasons. Firstly, Michelle had this niche for trying to be 'lovey dovey' when she thought I was doing something right. I wasn't feeling it. I wasn't some dog, who when she clicked her fingers I would come running. Secondly, I was bang on meeting Gemma. Really, I should have been trying to fight for my relationship but I really couldn't be bothered. I responded to Michelle. "I'm going out for drinks with the people from work", I said. "Oh", she replied. I could hear the disappointment in her voice but I couldn't give a shit. I was doing what I wanted when I wanted. "I will be back late so don't wait up for me", I said. "Ok", she replied in a rejected tone. "I love you", she added. "Ditto", I replied. Women or should I say Michelle, had a knack of saying "I love you" when I or men go out without them. Do they think we're just going to forget about them? In this case, I was but, it was just mad that they would say it on those occasions, rather than those times, when it was the two of you, or maybe my relationship had disintegrated so badly, it could not be fixed?

I met Gemma at Liverpool Street at around 6.13pm. Looking stunning in her pinstripe suit, we made our way down to Hoxton for drinks. The evening went well, as the evening seemed to last for ages. Gemma was a nice girl. As I said before she was a copper who stuck to the law. She told me it was the right of the British citizen to know the British law. I could tell she liked the power she had being a copper. "I don't pay for public transport", she said. "How come?" I asked. She cleared her throat and took a sip of her drink. "When you are a copper, you just show them your badge and they let you on", she claimed. I nodded my head in acknowledgement. After another sip on her drink, Gemma made another point that threw me. "You should join the force. They're looking for Black guys and other ethnic minorities to join the force", she said. She obviously didn't know that we (Black people) didn't have good relations with the Babylon. Brixton riots, the injustice of the Stephen Lawrence case, the list could go. Why would Black people want to work for an institution that constantly fucked them over? I looked at Gemma and told her it was not my cup of tea. She looked disappointed when I told her this. There was no way I could work for a racist institution such as the police. Fuck that. I'm sure Gemma had 'stopped and searched' a few 'niggas' but I didn't ask her that. I hated the feds. They let Stephen Lawrence's killers slip through the net. They even sent emails of a Black man decapitated around each other. I saw how the feds looked at me, even when I was in a suit. They all think that we are the same. The police don't keep law and order. They keep the Black man in check just like slave owners did their slaves back in the day.

The conversation then moved to me. Gemma asked me about my job. I told her about what I did and how a gay guy was helping me out. She laughed. "Gay guys are cool. They are good guys to have as gossip mongers, even if they have lied to me", she said. I was perplexed by her passing comment. "Did you have a bad experience with one?" I asked, knowing too well that was the case for me. Gemma took a deep breath, and then sighed. She seemed to tense up. "I shouldn't be telling you this, but I caught one of my ex boyfriends fucking a man" She said. I was shocked. "That's deep!" I proclaimed. She took a big swig of her drink, and lit her cigarette. Taking a big pull from the cigarette, she let out a cloud of smoke, and continued her story. "I loved that guy. I thought he loved me as well. I gave him my all literally, and then he screwed me by fucking a man! Gemma was clearly hurt by this guy's actions. She took another pull on the cigarette. "I knew he was feminine but not gay!" she exclaimed. I was speechless. Myself and Gemma had another thing in common; bad experiences with gays. "What did you do?" I asked. Clearly agitated by my probing, she took another large swig from her drink. "I just went for him. I hit, kicked, punched and scratched him. He was a skinny mix race guy who couldn't do shit. The other guy grabbed his stuff. Nate tried to restrain me but I wasn't having it". Gemma paused to light another cigarette. She took a steady pull on it. "I threw all of his stuff out", she added. She took another pull on the cigarette. "I changed all the locks on my door. He tried calling me, but I wasn't having it. I will NEVER forgive him for that!" she protested. Gemma grabbed her glass of Rose and drank it down in one gulp. "Shall we get another bottle?" she asked. I nodded my head in approval. I was about to get up when Gemma interjected, as she said she was going to get it. She went to the toilet first. I think the story about her ex upset her. This is because when she came back to the table, even though he had redone her make up, it was clearly visible to me that she had been crying.

We drank our third bottle of Rose. At this time, we were both tipsy. Gemma looked a lot happier. Maybe it was the drink or maybe I made her laugh after that story. Whatever had happened, she was a lot perkier. The bar we were in got more lively, and the music was blaring. I asked her if she fancied a dance. Gemma came closer to me and whispered into my ear that she wanted a shag! With that thought implanted in my cranium, we got our stuff and left the bar. We got a Black cab from Liverpool Street to Streatham. Whilst we were in the back of the taxi, we were kissing and caressing each other. She squeezed my dick as I sunk my mouth on to her big breasts. The taxi driver was clearly getting more than an eyeful. He was getting his money's worth. We pulled up to Gemma's flat in Streatham. I paid the taxi driver. We walked up to her flat, up the stairs and into her flat. No sooner had the door shut, it was on again. We were both kissing each other frantically like our lives depended on it. We moved to her lounge onto the sofa. We were ripping off each other's clothes until I was down to my boxers and she was in her red bra and thong. I was turned on by her lingerie. I rubbed my hand on her pussy with the thong on. She moaned wildly. I sat her on the sofa and pulled off her thong as we were kissing. Her pussy was hairy, just the way I liked it. If there was bush on the park, then you could play. Gemma took my boxers off and put her big lips onto my hard shaft. She then proceeded to suck it looking deeply into my eyes. Gemma was so much more experienced than Michelle and it showed. My dick got harder in her mouth. I wanted to fuck her. I whispered into her ear, "Do you want me to fuck you?" She whispered back into my ear 'yes'. Gemma slipped off her bra and came back to me. We started kissing again. I held her as I lay her down onto the sofa. I put my dick in her and started fucking her. She loved it. She was all kissing me and putting her hands all over me. I gave Gemma some fucking that night. I fucked her 'leg foot pon shoulder' and missionary. I doggied her over the sofa. Gemma was very flexible. She was like a lithe ballet dancer. We even shared a '69er' together. All these times I was licking her, she was kissing me and I was kissing her back. It felt good to be given love like that or give someone a good seeing to. I must have made Gemma cum numerous occasions. Her white voluptuous body did it for me. The long hair, the big breasts, the big hips and chunky thighs drove me crazy. It was a case of Othello. I was the beast with the two backs tapping this racist's daughter. Our bodies interwined were a reflection of Ebony and Ivory meeting each other for the first time. When I thrust myself into Gemma, she moaned and screamed. The variations of positions caused to say 'Oh Michael! Or 'Fuck me harder' or 'send me your soldiers'. I could fuck Gemma how I wanted. The sex was better with Gemma than Michelle. It wasn't so one sided or like a routine. It was spontaneous, exciting and refreshing. By the end of our session, I was 'cream crackered'. As Gemma lay on my chest, I smoked a fat 'zoot'. Good sex and a good spliff, I was blessed. After I smoked the 'zoot', I looked at my watch. It was 2.50am. I would have to get to Michelle. I didn't want to leave Gemma, but it would be 'bait' if I stayed out all night. I wrote a note and left it on her bedside table. I got changed quickly. I shut her front door quietly. I left her home smiling and knowing too well, I had a caught a large case of Jungle fever...

Chapter 12 Gemma

It was Saturday morning. The birds were tweeting and the light was shining through my room. I felt radiant and refreshed. After all, I did get a good shagging last night. Speaking of that, where was my young Black stallion so I could get a good seeing too again? I turned over, but he was gone! I looked over and saw a note on my bedside table. I picked it up. It read "Hiya Babes. Sorry I had to dash, got a few things to sort out today. I had a really good time last night- I knew there was something about you, you naughty minx lol. I will ring you later, Michael". I put the note back down. I had mixed emotions at this point. I was disappointed that Michael had gone. I was looking forward to more loving, more cuddling, breakfast in bed and chilling, watching DVDs. I missed his company and companionship that being a relationship bought. Conversely, being single, I found solace in fucking men I hardly knew, so it wasn't surprising when guys got what they wanted and literally fucked off. However there was something about Michael. I liked the fact that he called me a 'naughty minx'. I haven't had a good shag like that in ages. Michael knew what he was doing and what I liked. He wasn't selfish in bed. I mean how many guys lick pussy on the first fuck. I didn't know many that did that, and that was a sign to me that he would be coming back for more of this 'kitty kat', 'miaow'. Michael was caring. He didn't just fuck me and roll over. He made love to me and cuddled me afterwards. Unfortunately, us women release oestrogen after sex leaving us emotional, needy and vulnerable. Thank God for Cosmopolitan.

I sat up in bed and lit a fag. I wanted to reminisce about our session together. I could still smell Michael all over me. He was on my breasts, arms, legs, face and my pussy. I took a drag on my cigarette and relaxed as the nicotine entered my system. I smiled at the fact that Michael called me a 'naughty minx'. Fucking is like tangoing. You need two people to do it. He fucked me, and I sure fucked him. I knew this, because my belly, thighs and pussy were all aching. It's not just men who got to deliver the goods. Us, women have to do it as well. I know those ones when your girlfriends tell you that their guys left them because they were not fucking them right, or just laying there like a dead corpse. I remember riding Michael. I could see the glee in his face as I slid up and down his big black dick, with him loving it and squeezing my breasts. I missed him. There was a connection between us and it wasn't just a sexual one or was it? We got along, had a laugh, liked the same things, but the sex, it was just the one. I got my phone out of my bag, and decided to text him.

"Just thought I would text you to say thank you for a lovely evening. I look forward to seeing you soon. Take care from your naughty minx lol"

I sent the text, and got out of bed. I walked to the bathroom and ran a hot bath, so that I could commence with my day.

Chapter 13 Michelle

"OH SHIT!" Those were the words that echoed in my bathroom. I stood there visibly shaken. My world, my life, my destiny was going to change. I paced around the bathroom, like a mental patient in a psychiatric ward. It was like my world had caved in. Everything felt surreal. Nothing else seemed to exist or matter. I sat on the toilet staring at the instrument on the sink. I wanted to be sick. This should be one of the most exciting days of my life, but it really wasn't. I started to panic. Sweat poured down my face. Everything started to make sense. The constant vomiting, the constant trips to the loo and now this. It was official. I was pregnant. I was pregnant to a man that I didn't love anymore or want to be with anymore. Furthermore, was it his anyway?

I washed my face and looked in the mirror. I was going to be a mother or was I? I could have an abortion couldn't I? It was the easy route out of this? I was placed in a moral dilemma. Did I want to become another statistic and be a single parent with a baby father or have a sly abortion and carry on with my life? Moreover, should I keep the baby and try and make a go of my failing relationship with Michael? All these options teased my brain with such mystery and intrigue. Could I put myself through an abortion? A termination could jeopardise my chances of having a baby later on in life? The thought of losing my baby made me cringe and I held my stomach tightly. Tears started to run down my cheeks. I really didn't know what to do. At that point Ola came into my head. Could I leave Michael for Ola, whilst I was pregnant? Ola had been begging me to leave Michael from the time we kissed and had sex. I knew it was wrong, but Ola made me feel good about myself. He made me feel special just like Michael used to, but all of that was going to change. I couldn't have either man bringing up the other man's child or could I? No one would have to know. I would have to stop this mad rationing and regain my composure and focus. I wiped the tears from my face. I had to tell Michael that I was having his baby. I called him. "Michael", I shouted from the top of my voice. I heard him running up the stairs. "What's up?" he asked. "I got something to tell you", I said anxiously. Michael looked perplexed. "Come on spit it out!" he barked. My heart started to beat faster. My mouth had turned parched and dry. I stuttered "I'm, I'm, I'm", the words couldn't come out. Something so simple to say took ages now to come to light. Michael was getting agitated. "What is it! Tell me! You're scaring me!" he protested. He grabbed me. "I'm pregnant" I retorted. "Pregnant?!" he said back. I nodded and showed him the pregnancy test kit. He looked confused. "Say something then", I gesticulated. "What do you want me to say?!" He responded. "Are you happy, are you vex?" I asked. He now started to stutter. "Are, are you?" I was in two minds at this point. I replied "Yes, I am". Michael came to me and hugged me. I seemed to sort of melt into his body. It felt good to be in his arms and warmth. It felt like old times that I yearned for, but there was still a sense of uncertainty on my part. Michael would be a good Dad, but was he still the one for me? My encounter with Ola was obviously a reflection that he wasn't the one. However, we could try and make things right for the baby couldn't we? As we stood their hugging, I stared straight into the mirror. The uncertainty was etched in my countenance. My journey with Michael Brown had taken another direction, and I wasn't sure if I wanted to make this journey with him...

Chapter 14 Michael

I was thrilled with the prospect of being a father for the first time. No matter how exciting it was, it was also a tad daunting. There was a sense of going into the unknown which I didn't like, but I suppose every aspect of life is like that. To think that another version of me would be coming into the world. Would it be a boy? Would it be a girl? I didn't care, as long as my child was born healthy that's what mattered to me.

They say women are broody creatures. I say men can be broody too. A lot of my boys had 'yutes', and I suppose sub consciously it 'bun' me that I didn't have any kids to show. However that wasn't such a bad thing. Did I really want XYZ of baby mothers floating around? Did I want to be babysitting when I could be raving with my boys? Did I want to be buying pampers and all the other baby accessories? Also, when I looked at the situation that had been presented to me, I was in a different position to the majority of my boys that had kids. I was different to them because I was going in a different direction to them. However this was going to change, as I was going to be like them. I was going to be a daddy too!

Michelle was playing on my mind. Let's not lie about it; I had 'breeded' her up. Our relationship had been dire and maybe her being pregnant was the kick-start that we needed to revitalise our flagging relationship. Prior to Michelle becoming pregnant, she was quite distant with me. Maybe she was going through her own shit. Maybe she was cheating on me? I didn't rule that out as she often didn't want sex with me or sex was a 'quick ting'. I was still reeling over the news of Michelle's pregnancy when I got a text message on my phone. The vibrating sound startled me as I reached for the mobile device. I looked on the phone. It read "1 message received". I opened the text. It was Gemma. The text read

"Are we still linking up Baby? I'm missing you like crazy".

I didn't even bother to reply. I put the phone back in my pocket. I sat on the chair. This was mad. It still hadn't sunk in. I was going to a Dad. The happiness, confusion and disarray made me want to bill up a 'zoot'. Weed always seemed to numb any pain or madness. It was always a short term escape for me. However, after I stopped being lean, my problems would still be there and my perception of things would still be cloudy, if not, even more hazy. There were many times I had stop blazing and it would always do me good. My head would always be clearer. I wasn't paranoid. I didn't want to bang anyone over of the stupidest thing. My lips weren't black and I didn't have bags and impurities under my eyes. Fuck it! I wanted a 'zoot' and I wanted it now! As I was billing up my 'zoot', my phone stated to 'pop off'. It was Nathan, the guy from work. He asked if I fancied meeting up for a drink. He sounded down. I sounded down too. I thought why not. A 'zoot' and a drink to drown my sorrows. Not a good combination, but fuck it, I needed some air and I needed to get out in the open. Who would have thought that the evening would turn out so eventful...?

Chapter 15 Michael

I met Nathan at a bar in Liverpool Street that city workers often frequented. I spotted Nathan from a distance. He was leaning against a lamppost, smoking a cigarette, looking very fazed. His pint of Guinness was nearly finished. Upon seeing this, I went to the bar to buy another two pints. As I made my way to the bar, Nathan spotted me and I stood opposite him.

"I was just about to ring you. You took your time getting here",

"Traffic"

I was still visibly moved by the notion of being a 'Dad'. Nathan and myself proceeded to talk. It had merged that Nathan's boyfriend had dumped him. He had left Nathan for another guy. "He was fucking me and that bastard", Nathan protested. I was taken aback by this comment, primarily due to the fact that I didn't realize homosexuals had the same love problems as heterosexuals. Call it ignorance or maybe even naivety, or that I was caught up in my own drama to be giving a flying fuck how this 'battyman's' love life was crumbling by the edges. Nathan continued his angst. Paul, Nathan's now ex boyfriend was being a 'player' for a little while now, a few months to be precise. I could see why Nathan was pissed. I would be pissed as well if Michelle was doing that to me. However, I wasn't in a position to say anything, as it wasn't like I was being faithful, was I? I was any contradicting hypocrite who seemed to watch the world go by me day by day. At that point, I listened intently as Nathan continued. Paul was the guy that pulled Nathan out of a 'black hole'. Nathan used to be a rent boy, hooked on coke. His life was spiralling miserably out of control until Paul came into his life, and 'saved' him. "He made me feel good about myself", Nathan protested. He took a sip of his pint, and continued his story. He took a deep breath. "When I was doing all that fucked up shit just to survive and getting cheap kicks, Paul showed me that I didn't need to do all of that stuff", he said. I interjected at this point.

"So did he tell you why he left you for another guy?"

"Yeah he did"

Nathan paused as he took another sip from his pint of Guinness.

"He said I was too emotional and needy. Said I was too clingy to him and didn't give him enough space".

At that point, he started to cry violently like a bitch. I other on the other hand wanted to clap him in his face and tell him to 'man the fuck up'. I couldn't do that because he was hurt and I didn't think that gay men could 'man the fuck up', as they were so feminine. I took some tissues and gave them to him. Nathan wiped his tears from his face. I went over to him and gave him a reassuring arm round the shoulder. I genuinely felt sorry for him. He smiled, at my gesture. "Thanks for being supportive bro. It's much appreciated" he said. At this point Nathan regained his composure, and made his way to the toilet to sort himself out. When he came back, I had one of the deepest conversations that I had with anyone in my life.

Nathan said from day one that he was gay but just like the majority of people including myself, he decided to stay in the closet. His father, a Ghanaian man tried to always toughen him up, whilst his Irish mother thought it was lovely that her son was in touch with his feminine side. However, little did she know that her little boy was doing things that she would never believe? I asked Nathan if he ever had any girlfriends. He said he had a few but they were a cover up to his parents. He said he had one meaningful relationship with a girl called Gemma, and he nicknamed her 'Ice Gem'. He named her this after the sweet kids snack on and also that she could be cold as ice.

"I really fucked up there",

"What did you do?"

"Are you sure you want to know?"

Me being the nosy person that I was said "I'm not in no rush". It emerged that Nathan had been with Ice Gem for a little while, enough time to think that he might not be gay. "I somehow connected with her sexually. She had plump breasts and could ride me well", Nathan said excitedly, as if he was reliving a moment that they had shared. I laughed as I couldn't this skinny mixed race guy being dominated by this chic. Nathan said the relationship turned sour when he didn't have a job and was basically living off her. "I just got high everyday and watched daytime TV" he added. Nathan's previous life mirrored my previous life when I couldn't find a job. I could relate to this 'battyman' in so many instances, yet I preferred to distance myself from this notion as I didn't want to consider myself as one of 'them'.

"So what triggered the bust up then?"

I sounded like one of those tabloid journalists who was looking for a major scoop.

"The Internet",

I looked at him perplexed. Nathan explained when he and Ice Gem argued; he would feel insecure about himself and revert into 'gay' mode. The arguments made him question his sexuality to the point that he was going on gay porn sites, bashing off and then feeling guilty. I really wanted to reach out to him as I had experienced that too, but I didn't want to blow my cover story say to speak. That was my own dark secret that I didn't want to share with anyone, not even a priest in confession. Nathan continued his story. He claimed the more arguments he and Ice Gem had, the more he felt compelled to go on the net and look at gay porn. However, one day, that all changed.

"One day I decided to join a gay cruising site, as I didn't want to just masturbate anymore, I wanted to get back in the game",

The plot was thickening, and I, the tabloid journalist was eager to tease out this big story. It merged that Nathan put a profile of himself on this website so that he could find men to fuck from the net. That was crazy.

"So I take it you got lucky then?"

"Yeah I did, but it would cost me regrettably".

Nathan had met a black guy who wanted the same things as him. They spoke a couple times on msn, the site and the phone.

"We decided to meet up at my house. I planned it perfectly so I thought. Gem was going to be at work and I would have the house to ourselves"

"You got busted!"

Nathan nodded his head.

"What happened?"

The juicy bits were coming to light and I would have my big story. Nathan continued his story. "One day Gem was working late, so I decided to call the guy over". I was so amazed at Nathan's brazenness and sheer audacity to bring his next sexual partner into his current partner's home. Nathan lit a cigarette, and continued his story. "He was dark and muscular. We both knew what we wanted and didn't waste no time in achieving it". I was dumbstruck that someone could openly do something like that.

"I was getting the best rogering of my life, when I heard the bedroom door burst wide open. It was Gem",

"Shame"

Nathan took another sip from his pint. He continued his story.

"She just stood there with shock, dismay and disgust. For that moment, I wished the ground could swallow me up",

I was hooked by his story.

"Baby I can explain. She wasn't listening. She clean punched me in my face and I fell off the bed. The Black guy was getting his stuff, when Gem threw a vase towards him, screaming abuse"

49

"What did she say?"

"She called us fucking faggots. The vase narrowly missed him as he made it through the door. She was in absolute rage",

Nathan took a pull on his previously lit cigarette.   Nathan continued his story.

"She tipped the whole bedroom apart. I tried to restrain her, but she wasn't having it. She called me a dirty faggot. She said she could see me fucking another woman, but a man was a big no no!"

"What happened next?"

Nathan drew a deep breath. He began,

"After she calmed down, she told me to leave and never come back. I must have gone to my mate's house to crash, but didn't explain the situation. Next morning, I went back to Gem. Saw my stuff in black bags. My stereo was broken just like my playstation 2".

I saw the pain etched in Nathan's face. Nathan began to talk again. "I tried knocking the door a couple of times and ringing her phone but to no avail", Nathan said. A tear rolled down his cheek. He was an emotional guy.

"You don't realise you have a good thing until it's gone",

"Awoo",

"My life went downhill after that",

It was my turn to sip my drink and got prepared for what Nathan said next. Nothing even seemed to shock me when this guy spoke.

"I was homeless, couldn't crash at my mates all the time. I had to think how I could get some easy money. Then it came to me. I would become a rent boy",

"A rent boy?!"

I nearly choked on my drink. A rent boy I thought. How degrading. My next question to Nathan was "Why?" "Why on God's green earth would you subject yourself to such a thing?" I asked him. "It was easy money. I was getting paid for doing something I enjoyed", Nathan replied. I did not want to imagine Nathan doing what he had gone, but it was different strokes for different folks. Each to their own. It made me think when someone else is in unfortunate circumstances; you appreciate more the things you have in your own life.

It emerged that Nathan's life as a rent boy was one that you would expect in the world of vice. It consisted of upmarket clientele, designer garments, cocaine, speed, and shitting on MPs whilst they wore an Arsenal football shit, no pun intended. Nathan's life was this, but it came at a price. "I started to lose myself. Didn't know who I was anymore. For sure the reward of the job had its perks, but was this what life was cracked up to be?" Nathan pondered philosophically. Nathan's life cresended into a downward spiral. His cocaine habit was one that cost him his flat. "I was so desperate for a fix, I would use my rent money for some of the 'white stuff'", he protested. Nathan lit a fag. I could tell he was in a reflective mood. He spoke again. "Before I knew it, I was homeless again, just like the time when Ice Gem kicked me out! I crashed at my mate's again trying to figure out how awfully wrong it had gone for me. At that point I had a realisation. It occurred to me that being gay and consuming in same sex relationships was ruining my life", Nathan said regrettably. Upon on hearing this, it brought my world crashing back down to Earth. There was only so much a person could be in denial, and to Nathan's credit, he reminded me why I had to have Apple pie and not fudge. To me, fudge brought even more pain, drama, and anger than Apple pie. I took the last swig of my Guinness, and finally finished it promptly. My glass was empty. I felt Nathan's life was empty due to the decisions he had made and I didn't want to go down that same road. At that point Nathan interjected. "I then met Paul and everything seemed to change", he said. I could tell Nathan's story was lively again so

I decided to get myself and him a refill, as I knew things were going to get interesting again...

Chapter 16 Bar with Nathan (Michael)

"Paul was like my shinning knight of honour"
It emerged that Paul really did play a part in turning Nathan's sordid life around. He got Nathan off the drugs. Nathan moved in with Paul so he could get more stable. "I was also able to get a job", Nathan added as he took a drag ff his cigarette. As the toxic smoke filled his airways, he breathed out a cloudy array of fumes. "So what's happening with you?" Nathan cheekily asked me. I took a pause and slipped on my new pint of Guinness. I liked my Irish stout. It helped me fuck all night! It was now my turn to take a deep breath, as I started my story.
"Michelle's pregnant",
"Congratulations"
"Thanks"
"You don't seem too chuffed"
"I am and I'm not"
I could see the intrigue in Nathan's face. The attention had now been placed on me. Nathan liked that a lot, but being the 'battyman', I thought he would have been a drag queen and lapped all the attention up for its worth. I took a deep breath. I started to speak.
"I'm happy because I want to be a Dad"
"Ditto"
At that point, I couldn't imagine Nathan being a father, but this was the new norm. First gay men had the right to marry, and now they were adopting kids. It was a made state of affairs. I flipped the script with my next comment. I took a deep draw on my fag (no pun intended) and breathed a big cloud of smoke.
"I am not happy with the state of my relationship with Michelle and I don't want a baby brought into that",
Nathan looked at me with deep thought attached to his countenance.

"That's deep dude! You have proper thought this through".

"Yeah"

"Maybe the baby will bring you better times than you have now"

He gave me a reassuring smile. He continued. "Fuck it, let's celebrate!", and with that he was by the bar. When he came back he had two glasses and a bottle of champagne. "What are you doing?" I enquired. Nathan placed the two glasses and the bottle of champagne down on the table. He filled up both glasses. "We are celebrating", he said. He gave me a glass of champagne. Nathan spoke again. "We are celebrating me being single and you being a father". I thought Nathan was a crazy guy, but rather than bring his hype down, I joined him in celebrating our 'double joy'. Our 'double joy' was two contrasts juxtaposed together. Nathan was free. I wasn't. He could 'mash' as many guys as he could. I wouldn't be 'mashing' Michelle for a few months at least or any chick for that matter, as I would be changing nappies and playing happy families.

As the evening progressed and the drink flowed, I started to learn more about Nathan. We did have more in common that I previously had thought. One thing we did have in common was music. We liked the same types of music such as hip hop, garage, funky house, reggae, ska, you name it we both liked it. Then it came out. Nathan used to mc. I nearly choked on my champagne. "Just because I am gay, don't mean I can spit", he snorted aggressively. And with that he 'spat' a 16 bar. As Nathan 'spat' the aggressiveness in his delivery seemed to reflect his mood and his masculinity. I was impressed. Not to be outdone, I spat a 16 bar too. Coming from South London, and the time when 'So Solid' were still running tings, what Black guy couldn't say that they didn't mc. Nathan was impressed. He smiled as if to say I was 'big'. A mutual respect had been gained here.

"So how come you stopped spitting?" I asked curiously.

"Because I got lazy, other distractions and because I am gay",

I could see the disappointment etched in his face, as he sipped the champers from his glass. He took a pull from his cigarette. "I don't think the scene could handle a 'battyman mc', Nathan said. As much as I wanted to crack up with laughter, he had made a good point and I nodded my head in agreement. Just like the bashment scene, garage mc's and fans were not tolerant of 'chi chi' men, let alone a 'chi chi' mc. I could see it now in a rave, if people knew Nathan was gay and he 'spat'. He would have gun fingers pointed at him by guys and girls for that matter, flashing lighters and singing in unison "Bun off the chi chi". Being gay was a hindrance and an unnecessary hindrance that I didn't need in my life.

"I would have made money if I became a successful mc"

Nathan piped in. I wanted to say 'no' but my mother had instilled in me that you must always think before you speak. I retracted my trail of thought. Nathan would have made bare cash, as the A and R's of record labels would have loved to sign a gay mc. They would want one that talked about being gay, being in love and being shafted by guys. It would have been a good marketing tool for these rich music companies. Nathan being this gay mc would pay for them having ostentatious goods, going to A' list parties and more chances to hoover up 'white' up their hooters. I chuckled to myself as I said 'yes' in agreement to Nathan being possibly a successful gay mc.

I looked at the table. The champers was finished. Our glasses were empty. I looked at my watch. It was 12.33 am. It was early. I wanted to get lashed.

"You up for the lash?"

"You've changed your tune. I thought it was just a quiet few"

I looked around at my surroundings. The bar had got lively. The ambiance of the bar has improved dramatically just like my aura. The music had got louder. There were suddenly more women in the facility. I could openly flirt with them. It would be better than going home to a pregnant Michelle who would be too tired or not in the mood for sex. More importantly I was enjoying the stimulating conversation with Nathan, and I was enjoying his company.

"I'm gonna get a few drinks to get us lashed"

"Go for it"

I was too fixated on a mix race woman at the bar. Alcohol made me horny and I wanted to 'mash'. I couldn't 'chirps' this woman. For God sake, I was going to be a Dad. However my bad side was telling to chat to the woman, so I could get her number and then proceed to fuck her. I wasn't getting no loving from the woman that I was supposed to love, so why not. Just as I was about to get up and make my move, Nathan came with a tray of different drinks. The tray had pints of Guinness, cider, along with shots of tequila and sambucca.

"This will get us shit-faced"

"Hell yeah",

It was probably a good thing that Nathan came at that moment. He prevented me from having more stress in my life or did he?

Myself and Nathan started to get through the drinks. We had drunk the Guinness and now on the tequila. We got through them in a swift. We still had the sambuccas and the two pints of cider each to drink. The time was now minutes to two. I enjoyed Nathan's company. He made feel relaxed and calm. I could be myself and not have to watch my 'p's and 'q's around him. Just like the tequila, we got through the sambucca shots like we were in a race. It was at this point three things happened. I started to feel drunk, my mood changed and that question was asked.

"For someone is going to be a father, you don't look happy?"

I took a long pause and looked at Nathan. I got my pint of cider and downed it in one. Nathan looked on in awe. He giggled in his camp laugh. I was drunk now and the truth emerged. I slurred my words.

"I am Daddy, have girl on side, getting no sex and top of that, I might be gay".

"You what?! Say that last bit again"

Being drunk, I reached for my last pint of cider and took a big sip from it. The truth was fast merging. I took a deep breath. "I think I might be gay!" I said. Nathan looked amazed at my admission. The drink in my system seemed to let me relax. The words seemed to just flow from my tongue. I told Nathan everything from how feelings came about sinning, websites, Amsterdam. In my drunken state, I sensed Nathan felt more comfortable knowing that someone else had gone through a similar experience to him. By the end of the night, I had gone from this sober frustrated guy to this drunk and horny man. I was ready to go home. I was ready to go home and fuck.

"You can stay at mine if you want?"

Nathan had put me in a position. I was pissed out of my head and said 'yes'. A part of me remembered that I had a pregnant girlfriend at home waiting for me. I called Michelle. It rang a bit, and then she answered. "Hello", she said in a half sleep, half awake tone. "It me", I slurred. "Umm", she replied back. "I'm staying at Nathan's" I slurred again. "Ok", she replied, and with that she put the phone down. Nathan and I staggered out of the bar after 3. We were both wasted. We were swaying like pirates on a ship that been hit by turbulence. We were enjoying the moment, laughing away liked we cared about nothing in the world. My phone then vibrated. I took my phone from my pocket. It was a text. I opened the text, expected it to be from Michelle. However it was from Gemma. The text read

"Miss you xxx"

I didn't reply. I was too drunk to do so. Her text meant that she was lonely and needed loving. I could have gone to hers but that would have been 'dark' on Nathan. Maybe, I should have gone there that night, as if I had, I would have had 2 dramas instead of 3 to deal with. Just then, I heard someone shout from the top of their voice my name. "Come on Michael!" It was Nathan. He got us a taxi. I walked up to him and slapped his bottom as he got into the cab. He laughed drunkenly and smiled at me if to say it was ok to do that. I stumbled into the cab, as Nathan told the cab driver where we going. As the taxi travelled to Nathan's house, the two of us started play fighting in the back. I could see the taxi driver getting annoyed in his rear mirror. Then I did something that would change my life forever. I did something that would change my relationship with Nathan... I kissed him full blown on the lips. I expected Nathan to pull away, but he didn't. This surprised me, but then it didn't as we were both drunk. As we embraced each other passionately, I could see the disgust in the taxi driver's face. Fucking bigot I thought. His reaction drove me further in my embrace with Nathan. I put my hand in Nathan's trousers and started to wank him. He loved it as he groaned. Before we knew it, we had reached the end of our destination. We had reached Nathan's house. We got out of the taxi. I paid the taxi driver, smirking at him. He still had that look of disgust on his face. "Fucking fagots", he retorted as I walked from the taxi. "You what?!" I barked who was this prick to call me a faggot?! He didn't know me or what I was capable of. I kicked his taxi in anger. "I don't want any trouble", he shrieked. "Yeah", I thought. You're fucked now. I thought. This taxi man had this angry Black man ready to 'buss' his ass. In Jamaica, it was a big thing to call someone a 'battyman' and try get away with it. Guys have been killed for that. Didn't he know that careless talk cost lives?! At that point Nathan dragged me away, and told the taxi man to promptly 'fuck off'. He did promptly; most probably relived he didn't hold an arse whooping in the road.

We walked into Nathan's place. I was still drunk and still seething from that remark. Nathan bought me over a whisky to calm me down.

"I have never seen you like that before",

"It's nothing ",

I gulped down all the whisky, whilst Nathan finished his cigarette.

"I like you angry, you look sexy",

Nathan squeezed my thigh. I perked up at that. The thought of pounding this faggot and teaching him a lesson turned me on. I grabbed Nathan and kissed him passionately. He grabbed my hand and led me to his room, shutting the door firmly.

Chapter 17 Michael

I woke up with a dirty hangover. My head was spinning next levels. I looked to see where I was. I felt very disorientated due to the sheer mass of alcohol that I had consumed the previous night. I was in a bed in a room that I didn't recognize. I looked around more to see if I could get my bearings. I looked to my left and I saw a picture of Nathan. I felt relived. I must have crashed at Nathan's place. I had a duvet on me, but my balls felt chilly. I took a look beneath the duvet to see my bollocks out of door. I started to panic. Why was I naked? I looked around furthermore. I saw my clothes and Nathan's clothes sprawled across the ground. At that point, I experienced a flashback of the evening before. I remembered arguing with the taxi man, but nothing else. My mind was blank. My heart started to beat faster. Had I and Nathan fucked? I got out of the bed, and tried to find a condom. I couldn't. There were none on the floor, none in tissue, and none in the bin. I checked my wallet to see if I used the one I stored there. It was still intact. "Oh shit!" I uttered. I felt dirty. I felt like that experience in Dam again. I shuddered at the thought of it. I started to put on my clothes, my head still pounding from the night before. Once dressed, I went to the sink to wash my face. I looked in the mirror. I didn't recognize the dishellved man in the mirror. I knew one thing though. I needed to get out of here. I opened the door to see Nathan eating breakfast. He was smiling at me.

"Morning sleeping beauty!"

"Alright",

"Fancy some breakfast?"

I paused before I replied. I saw what was on Nathan's plate. The sight of two boiled eggs, a sausage between them with a splash of mayonnaise at the bottom of the sausage repulsed me and reminded me of the possible sodomy that may have occurred. "I will pass", I uttered. I pulled up a chair and sat at the table. Nathan was still smiling at me, whilst eating his 'two meat and veg'. "What did we do last night?" I asked. Nathan took his sausage of his plate, licked it, then proceeding to put the sausage in this mouth. He started to chew, and then swallow. He then looked at me. "We did everything", he replied gleefully. That was enough for me to leave. I got up immediately for the table and made a beeline for door. "Don't want to you stay for some more action?" Nathan asked smirking like the cat that got the cream. "No!" I shouted, as I grabbed my coat, opening the door, and slamming as I left. It had to be a drunken mistake, as I walked the roads. I felt dirty and confused. I felt like Dam all over again. I just wanted to go home, have a shower, feel clean and feel the love of a woman not a man. However, I knew that wasn't going happen at home as Michelle being pregnant didn't help. Also, she had become distant and displayed no affection towards me. It had been like this for some time. Just then I received a text message. I thought it was Nathan, but it turned out to be Gemma. The text read

"Are you ok?"

That was the thing about Gemma that I liked. She was consistent. I sent her a text back saying I would call her back later. The text made me feel manly again, however I still wanted to go home and wash away my 'sins'.

Chapter 18 Nathan

Dear Diary,

Something crazy happened last night. I never saw it coming to be honest, but I'm glad that it happened on both our parts. The black guy I work with, Michael, I slept with him. We went out to celebrate the end of my last relationship and his upcoming baby. As the night wore on, we got drunk and ended up at my house were things happened. I knew this wasn't his first gay experience by the way he touched and fucked me. He had done before it again. Also, his dick was huge. Not such a myth for Black guys then. However, Diary, I think I am falling for him big time. I never expected him to be gay, but it seems everyone is these days. He is such a sound guy. I feel so comfortable around him. I don't want this to be a drunken fling. I want to this to be the real deal. Michael stormed out of my flat. I don't think he can deal with being a closet gay, especially with a baby on the way. It is a deep one. I think if he came out, his life would be easier, and he could be with me. We could be happy and spend a lot of time together. I know we could work. He is the guy that I have been looking for a long time. I can't get him out of mind. His body, his dick, the way he fucks, and his personality. He's just perfect. My scheme has worked so far. I have turned him, but this was only stage one of my plan. I wouldn't expect him to leave his girlfriend and baby, but in the long run, he could come to me. I am so excited. I haven't felt like this before. I think I'm in love again...

Chapter 19 Work with Nathan (Michael)

Monday had come round so quickly. I hadn't spoken to Nathan since our encounter and was not looking forward to seeing him either at work. I had eschewed any possible encounter with him. However I couldn't keep on trying to duck him. I would have to deal with seeing him at some point. I got to work around 10 am. As I walked to my desk, I noticed Nathan was not at his desk. I felt relieved. I knew I had some photocopying to do, so I went to the photocopying room to deal with that. I hadn't started my photocopying when I felt someone squeeze my bum?! I turned around in shock to find Nathan standing behind me smiling. My face turned to utter disbelief. "How you hanging there big boy?" he asked brazenly. I was aghast at his actions. I saw red and grabbed him by his throat. "Forget about what happened it was a mistake", I angrily said. Nathan smiled. "You don't mean that, you are gay, deal with it", he uttered. This really infuriated me. I clenched my fist ready to deck him when I saw someone walk past the room. I let go of Nathan. I was greatly piqued by his sheer brazenness. "I like it when you're angry, you look so sexy", said Nathan. I didn't like the fact that he had one up on me. He could expose me. He could destroy me. The ball was in his court, but I wasn't prepared to rise to the bait. I walked off leaving him there. "You can't hide it bro!" he exclaimed. I knew that he was referring to my sexuality. I had to deal with it and thought I had closure, but obviously not. This prick was intent on making my life hell and making me his partner. Never that!

I kept my head low at work. I didn't want another altercation with that freak. Why couldn't that guy accept what happened was a mistake? At that point, an email flashed on my p.c. It was from that jerk Nathan. It read
"I am sorry about before, but I really want to be with you"

I deleted the email promptly. I left my desk immediately and went for a cigarette outside. As I smoked my cigarette, I tried to figure out how I could get this guy to leave me alone. Who would have thought Nathan would leave me alone eventually, but not in the unforeseeable circumstances that prevailed...

Chapter 20 Meeting with Gemma (Michael).

Having not seen Gemma for a while, we decided that I would come round for dinner, watch a DVD with a bottle of wine. I had got over that incident with Nathan, or that's what I wanted to convince myself, but it still played on my mine. I knew I had slipped up so badly. When I got home, I had a shower for a long time. Michelle was moaning that I was going to run out all the hot water, or maybe she was concerned that I was cheating? Nothing had really changed with Michelle. She was still distant with me. She was still picking arguments with me. She wasn't displaying any affection to me either. She was definitely getting bigger, more hormonal and more fatigued. One possibility was that Michelle was vexed with me for not spending anytime with her. In my defence, I found it hard to stay in the same room as her as she brought my 'mojo' down. I really didn't really want to dump her being pregnant, but it was rapidly getting to that point. I knew if I did this, people would say I wasn't being a responsible father, but I wouldn't let it come to that point.

As I got ready to go to Gemma's, Michelle asked me where I was going. I told that I was going to help Nathan with his p.c. She laughed. "Anyone would think you two were a couple the way you're always around there", Michelle said. I laughed nervously, as Michelle was obviously oblivious to my encounter with Nathan. Maybe Michelle assumed that I wasn't cheating as she didn't see a gay guy as a threat to my relationship with her. If only she knew. This is why people shouldn't make assumptions; you make an arse of yourself. I didn't even kiss Michelle as I knew she wouldn't respond or she would respond coldly. I said bye, she said bye, our relationship a mere comfort thing as the only thing keeping us together was our unborn baby.

As I was on the train to Gemma's, I got a text from her. It read,

"Can't wait to see you baby!"

I liked seeing Gemma. She was blatantly a form of escapism for me and she was all things that Michelle wasn't. I got to Michelle's house at 7.30pm. I sneaked a tester bottle of CK one and sprayed it on me. I backed a Wrigley's extra to make my breath smell fresh. It wasn't about Gemma telling me that my breath was harsh! I had a bottle of Rose in a plastic bag. I was all prepared. I knocked the door. Within a few seconds the door opened. A burly old bald white man opened the door. "What do you want? He grunted aggressively. "Is Gemma there?" I asked politely. This man looked me up and down. It was he like he was sizing me up. He poked his head around the door, and shouted "Gem, there's someone here for you", and with that he left me on the doorstep. "OK", I thought to myself. Seconds passed, and then Gemma arrived at the door. She was delighted to see me. "Hiya Babes", she greeted me. "Do come in", she said. I entered the flat with Gemma. The man who answered the door was putting his coat on. "I will be making a move", he muttered. "Have you met Michael?" she asked him. "Yeah", he replied uninterested or oblivious that Gemma was trying to introduce me to him. "This is my Dad", Gemma said. I offered out my hand to shake his. He looked at it and declined. "Sorry pal, old arthritis, finds it hard to shake hands". I could tell what type of guy I was dealing with. I had come across men like him many times before and refused to come down to their levels. "It's ok, I understand", I replied. He seemed surprised by my blasé response. Maybe he was expecting me to 'while out' on him, thus justifying one of the many dated stereotypes placed on young Black men. There was a moment of awkward silence. Gemma's Dad then kissed her on her forehead. "Remember what I said Gem", he said, and with that he left. I was glad that he gone as I could have my wicked way with his daughter. "Sorry about that", Gemma said. "What was that about?" I enquired, already knowing that her father was a clear racist. Gemma started to tell me the deal with her father. He had been mugged by a bunch of Black guys, and that left an impressionable mark on him. This really pissed me off about Black guys. They never seemed to realise that when they were shooting, 'jacking' and fucking people over, they were fucking things up for us decent Black guys out there. It was already difficult for us decent Black guys to make a mark out there without those dumb pricks making the process even more difficult. However, as a young Black guy myself; I could see why those guys were driven to jacking Gemma's Dad. Many of them were living in poverty driven estates with absent fathers. Their educational chances hampered as many teachers did not want to take a chance on them and had written them off as soon as they entered the classroom. Black boys had been denigrated by society. 'Shoting' drugs, jacking people and shooting people were the only means these young guys knew how to survive. Unfortunately, when the few of the minority fucked up, the entire majority felt they were all like that. "It's cool, cos I know you're not like that", I said. Gemma smiled. We made our way to the table, where Gemma had cooked dinner. As I sat at the table, I could see various awards, certificates and pictures of Gemma and her family. They were all based on her work with the Police. I remembered one picture distinctly stuck out. It was a picture of Gemma's late mother. It had candles around the picture. Gemma looked like her mum. That was where she got her good looks from and not her bigoted father.

The evening went really well. We had dinner, drank wine, watched DVDs, and cuddled up on the sofa. It was really nice. It reminded me of old times with Michelle. I wished we still had those times but I knew it wasn't to be. I enjoyed Gemma's company. Her place was escapism for me. The DVD we were watching was starting to drag on and get boring. I asked Gemma what was for dessert. She smiled cheekily. "Me" she said. With that she stopped the DVD and took off her clothes.

"I went lingerie shopping, hope you like"

I looked up and right before me, Gemma was standing right before me in this black and red thong and bra. My dick started to twitch when she bent down, showing off her fat pussy in that thong. My dick was now swollen. The big man was indeed ready for action. I grabbed Gemma from behind and started kissing her neck passionately. She moaned and groaned as I slipped my two fingers into her wet pussy. She loved it. She then uttered that she wanted my dick in her. I hadn't brought no condoms and the fact that my dick that I 'bare backed' someone's bum with, was now going bareback into someone's pussy. Fuck it, I would with any consequences later, but as fate had it, I would pay for my careless actions. I slipped my erect penis out my boxers. I bent Gemma over, sliding her thong to the side and my bare dick into her white wet pussy. I 'doggied' her lights out that night, slapping her bare buttocks with my hands. I finally bought her body close to me and I came in her. Both exhausted in the chair, we lay in unison in the sofa cuddled up. "I love you Michael. Please don't leave me", Gemma said. Slightly perturbed by this response, I replied, "I won't leave you". The irony here being Gemma would be the one leaving me...

Chapter 21, Gemma, Her Situation

I knew something wasn't right. The constant morning sickness and the wooziness was messing me up. I wasn't on the pill, and usually Michael would wear condoms. However on the last few occasions, Michael had not 'strapped' up. It was nice to feel him 'bareback' and even better when he came in me. The cum trickling down my thighs and legs made me laugh. Conversely, now wasn't the time to be laughing. I made a trip to the chemist and bought two pregnancy kits. I did the first one. It was weird pissing on a strip that would ultimately determine my fate. That minute felt like an eternity to come. I picked up the pregnancy kit. It was the positive strip. I was pregnant. I dropped the pregnancy kit on the floor. I was in utter shock. I was going to be having a 'Black' baby. What would Dad think? It was bad enough that he didn't like Black people and trouble accepting Michael, but he could accept that his grandchild would be 'half-caste'. I needed to be 100% sure that I was pregnant. I did a second pregnancy test. Again, it felt like an eternity for the result to come. I picked up the pregnancy kit. It was positive again. Tears started to run down my cheek. I wasn't sure if the tears were because I was happy or distraught, but were they tears of confusion? The lights in my bathroom started to flicker. Was this a sign? It made me nervous and agitated. My eyes were weeping and my body was shaking. I needed something to calm me down. I reached my bag for my cigarettes. I took one fag out of my Benson and Hedges gold box. I put the fag to my mouth and was about to light it, when the realisation hit me. I was pregnant and could no longer smoke for the next 9 months. I threw the cigarette down in disbelief. I still needed something to calm me down. I walked over to the drinks cabinet. I took out the bottle of brandy and poured some into a glass. This time I wasn't caring that I was pregnant, and wolfed it down the cup of brandy in one gulp. Fuck it; smoking would do more harm to the baby than alcohol. I felt the brandy warm my chest like warm coal fumes rising up a chimney. I sat down and sprawled out in my sofa. I lay there with one hand on my stomach. There was a being in me. I was pregnant, but more importantly, I was going to be a Mum. As I lay there contemplating motherhood, it dawned on me that I was going to have tell Michael our good news. I wanted to tell him face to face, but felt more at ease calling him and telling him over the phone. I called him.

"Hello Babes"

"Hi"

"I was thinking about you"

"Ok",

I replied all coy. I took a deep breath, all getting ready to tell him, when he quipped in with

"Babes is it ok to come over tonight? Had a hard day and need to distress".

"Ok",

"Ok, see you at 8. See you later Babes"

The phone went dead. Michael was gone. I didn't get to tell him. I lay back down on the sofa and fell asleep, trying to forget that I was having Michael's baby.

"BUZZ BUZZ". I was woken by the sound of the intercom. I felt woozy. I looked at the clock. It had just gone after 8. "BUZZ BUZZ". The intercom went off again. "Alright, alright", I shouted. It was most probably Michael. I went to the intercom. "HELLO", I said in an aggressive tone. "It's me", a chirpy voice replied. It was Michael. I let him in. The place was in darkness. I felt like shit. I could have done with more hours in the sack, but I had to 'face the music and dance' say to speak. I saw a large figure merge at my front door. I tuned the passage light on and opened the door. I walked back to the living room. It felt like a long walk back to the living room. I felt dejected, just like how the England football players must have felt as they trudged back to the changing rooms on that dark night when Croatia knocked them out of the qualifiers for Euro 2008. I sat down on the sofa, with my hands on my face, oblivious to the noise of shoes coming off someone's feet and the clattering sound of footsteps approaching my living room.

"Are you ok?"

"No"

I looked up and saw the concern on his well chiselled face. Michael was an airing and sensitive guy when he wanted to be. Bless him. I needed a hug badly and by Jobe, I needed it now! Michael sat on the sofa. I immediately clambered to him. "Just hold me tight", I said. Michael held me tight like I was a football being smothered into a goalkeeper's hands. Michael ran his hands through my hair. Would he be still sweet when I told him the news? I felt safe and protected when I was with Michael. A tear ran down my cheek, followed by another, and then a dozen. The two of us sat in unison, peace and harmony. Suddenly Michael perked up. He felt my tears on him. "Why are you crying Gemma?" he asked. I looked at him. He was so handsome and prestigious. Why would he want to be with me for? I was ugly, fat and pregnant?! I stared at him in his face. It seemed like an eternity for the words to come.

"I, I, I"

The words struggled to come from my mouth. I could see Michael getting concerned with me. "Its ok Babes, you can tell me", he reassured me. I took a deep breath. I took a deep breath. I started,

"I'm, RING, RING"

My telephone started to ring, at all moments to ring, why now?! "Don't you think you should answer it?" Michael asked. "It's most probably not important", I replied back. The phone stopped ringing. Michael looked back at me. "So you were saying darling, your?" he said. At this point, I was getting even more frustrated. Fuck it, I'm going to just going to say it. I blurted it out.

"I'm PREGNANT"

Michael paused. His Black face turned white. He looked like he had seen a ghost or the Grimm Reaper for that matter. He edged back and recoiled in the sofa. 'OK', I muttered to myself in my head. He's in shock, I'm sure he will come around.

"Say something",

"Is it mine?"

I had to take a double take there and then. I know he didn't just say that?! Did he think I was some loose slag who freed it up to anyone and anybody? This 'nigger' was taking the fucking piss. I was angry and irate and it showed. My face had had turned blue like thunder. "Of course it's fucking yours?!" I retorted as I clenched my fists, gritting my teeth with the desire to punch him in his 'nigger' face. Sensing my anger, Michael responded quickly. "I was just checking", he said. Did he not think I wouldn't get pissed off with that flippant remark?!

"Is that all you can say?!"

Michael didn't respond. He looked dumbfounded. He looked like he had been hit for six. He picked up my lighter and cigarettes and went to the balcony, shutting the door behind him. I watched as he lit the fag and muttered "No, this can't be happening", with his body hung over the balcony. Yes this was happening, and he better deal with it or else....!

Chapter 22-Nathan

"I'm so sorry to break that news to you my friend".

Those were the words that the nurse uttered to me at the clinic. These words would stay with me for the rest of my life. In my darkest hour, could God help me here? This was a test of faith, but I didn't think the Almighty could help me now. The nurse gave me some leaflets, some medication and another appointment card. I couldn't even cry. My life had shattered right there and there, and what for some bum sex. That's right, you guessed it. I had contracted the HIV virus. I hadn't been feeling well for a little while now, and went to the STI clinic just for safe regards. Who would have thought I would leave there with a death sentence. As I left the clinic, it started to rain. I looked to the Heavens and asked myself could God really wash away this sin, this plague? The rain started to pour down harder. To me the answer was no. My clothes were soaked from the rain. As I made that lonely walk to the bus stop, and I had to think of where and who did I get this ailment from. I had slept with so many men unprotected recently in the last few weeks. Could I have got it from the many men that fucked me at Chariots? Could I have got it from my rendezvous with Michael? Could I have got it from my shenanigans at The Locker Room? I just didn't know. None of these guys were a regular partner. There was no chance I could get with Michael. There was no way Paul would take me back. I had fucked up many times in my young life, but never like this before. I had been burnt before but not like this. I had caught Chlamydia before. I had caught Gonorrhoea before. I even contracted Syphilis. I had taken massive dosages of penicillin that hurt like mad in order to recover. Thus I was told to wrap it up. My Dad from what I vaguely remembered of him, always used to say, "Those who don't hear must feel!" I was definitely hearing now, but it was too late. I had been playing the AIDS lottery for a long time and never won the main prize, but now I had won the HIV prize for my troubles. My bus came and I got on it to go home.

I read the leaflets that the nurse gave me. I read stuff on the net but nothing was going to change. I was still HIV positive. I felt my belly make some hunger noises. There was some left over pizza from the night before from my date. Could he have given me HIV? I doubt it. We used condoms, but he was a shit lay so I deleted his number. So much for staying in touch. I didn't really have an appetite and anything I ate didn't really stay down, due to the constant diarrhoea I had acquired. My life was changing and I wasn't in control of it. That scared me, and it frustrated me. I threw a plate down in anger and it smashed it into many fragmented pieces. I started to cry uncontrollably and fell to the ground. I kept shouting "Why me?!" I picked up a piece of the fragmented plate. Those suicidal thoughts of yester year came into my temple to haunt me. I scratched a piece of the fragmented plate into my left wrist. I found it sadly therapeutic and soothing when blood drew from it. I stopped but this time the desire to continue was there, until loads of blood came strong. I kept on hacking away, but my hard skin was being stubborn. Only a bit of blood came from my arm. Frustrated with my blood thirsty ways, I stopped. I went to the fridge, with my arm dripping of blood. I didn't care anymore. I got a bottle of Rose that I had left and started to swig it from the bottle. Alcohol seemed to be my vice when times were tough. I was going to need lots of it. Suddenly Michael just popped into my head. This guy that I lusted for started to merge as a potential candidate. Could he have given me this life sentence? He was a player, a 'gyalis', a dirty dog, whatever you wanted to call him. He fucked me, he fucking some white bitch and he was fucking his long term 'wifey'. I knew he was a bareback rider, as he fucked me bareback. Yes he was the one that infected me; he was the one to blame. I picked up my mobile phone ready to cuss him off when it dawned on me that he was going to be a father to a child who would be unaware of its father's selfish ways. Why should it have to suffer for their father's misdemeanours? My mind completely changed. I couldn't cuss this guy I loved. I couldn't blame him for my witless ways. He wasn't to blame, I was. I took another swig from the bottle. I had to take Dutch courage. I was going to call him. Fuck it, I dialled his number. It rang a couple of times and he answered.

"Hello",

"Blood, its Nathan"

I could hear the irritation in his voice.

"What do you want?!"

"I think you should go the clinic. The doctors told me that I got HIV".

The line went dead. I don't if his battery or reception went dead or he put the phone down on me, but it was evident Michael was not a happy bunny. I tried calling him back, but it kept on going to voicemail. The more and more it went to voicemail, the more I got frustrated. I couldn't blame him for reacting the way he did, but I loved this guy and just wanted to make sure he was ok. I rang him a few more times and it was the same response. Then it happened. I wanted to end it now. Fuck the self harming; I wanted to go out another way. I ran to the bathroom, straight to the cabinet. There was a bottle of paracetamol. I took the bottle of paracetamol and a put a few in my mouth. I washed them down with the rest of the Rose. I lay down on the floor of the bathroom, and waited for my time on Earth to go and my ascension to Hell to happen...

Chapter 23: Michael

It had been a manic two weeks for me. I don't even know where to start. I know one thing though, I feel like shit and look like shit. The stress of the last two weeks has been too much for me. I haven't been sleeping well over the last 14 days. I have been blazing a lot. I mean chain smoking blazing, one zoot after the other. I would have one in the morning, a few at work, a few at home and one before bed. I have hardly eaten. My appetite hasn't been there. My hair is a mess. It looks overgrown and picky. My beard looks worse for wear. Weed just deals with my problems short term. It feels good to get high, but when I come off of it, my situation is still there and that fuels my desire for more Buddha. Michelle has sensed something is wrong, but she seems hesitant to approach me. Even before she became pregnant, we have become distant. Obviously since she has been pregnant, we haven't made love for a long time, but there's no affection, no "I love you's". It was times like these that I could do with that hug or that cuddle just to reaffirm to me that everything are going to be ok. However, it doesn't happen. I am much to blame for this than anyone else. If anything, it would be me to be the controller of my destiny and sort things out.

Everything started to go pear shaped when Gemma told me that she was pregnant with my child. When she told me, my face went numb with shock. I was now going to have two kids. A black child and a mix race child. How could this be? How could I be responsible for bringing a child that may feel they had the best of both worlds when really they wouldn't? For a start there was no way Gemma was going to call our child 'Jade' or 'Ashley', as these were typical mix race kids names. I didn't want to accept it, but if I was man enough to come in her, than I would have to be man enough to deal with the consequences. I reassured Gemma that I would be there for her and the child. I still don't think she believed me because she seemed to notion that I could move into her place so we could be a family?! I told her I would think about it. She looked disappointed by my response, but I couldn't for obvious reasons.

Gemma being pregnant was the first drama in that manic two weeks. I received a phone call from that 'faggot' Nathan. The phone call would shake me up and make me re-assess my life accordingly. The motherfucker told me he had contracted the HIV virus, and that I should get tested. I locked off the phone as I was devastated and worried that I could have this man made virus. I looked back at it now, and realise that the guy was decent to tell me what happened. I hadn't been able to look the guy in his face because I was so vex, but also I was disappointed and saddened that this had happened to someone I knew. So many thoughts had run through my head. Did I have HIV? Did my kids have HIV? Did Gemma and maybe Michelle have HIV? I was shit scared. I didn't want this death sentence on me. I didn't sleep at all that night Nathan told me that news. I was so restless, that I fell asleep on the sofa. I woke up to find a quilt on me.

I made an appointment at the STI clinic. I hated going there. I had been burnt before, so I should have learnt my lesson, but I hated wearing condoms, and liked to wet my Willy. However, there were no times for jokes. This was ultra-serious. Whenever I went clinic, there was always a high propensity of Black men in the waiting room. This was an obvious reflection of the highly sexual promiscuity of Black men, and their desire to be 'bareback riders'. My number was called out and I was escorted to a room with a nurse. The nurse asked me the usual questions. He then asked the dreaded question, 'Had I slept with a man?' It was this action that had led me to the clinic. I said 'yes' hesitantly. The nurse was impartial to any answer you gave. It was then time for the dreaded tests. Giving the urine samples for Chlamydia and the blood samples for HIV, AIDS and Syphilis were fine. I was ok with needles. Maybe I was a Heroin addict in a former life. I just hated taking the swabs from my dick. I was not used to something alien going into the inside of my dick. I couldn't look when the nurse inserted the two swabs into the tip of my penis. The feeling was so surreal and it hurt. After the tests, I went back to the waiting room. It seemed like a destiny to get called back to get the preliminary results. I could see other 'niggas' sweating over their results. Each brother had their own different story as to why they were at the clinic. My number was called again. I didn't have any of the minor STI's, but it would still take two weeks for the HIV/AIDS results to come back. I got the usual ticking off and a bag of condoms for my troubles.

I got home but the worries were still there. Did I have HIV? Would my kids have HIV? Did Gemma and Michelle have HIV? How would I face Nathan at work, if the results came back positive? It was a veil of madness. I felt so empty, so worthless, so dejected. Is this what my life was to epitomize? I pondered this as I got high on my sofa...

Chapter 24 Michael –Tinseltown

It had been 4 months since I had the HIV scare. I was so glad that the results had comeback negative. It gave me the inspiration to try and sort things out with Michelle, Nathan and Gemma. Things had got awkward at work with Nathan, so I took the opportunity to clear the air with him. Nathan had changed since he contracted HIV. He seemed to be a shadow of his former self. He looked tired and lost a lot of weight. He was the skinniest I had seen him. He wasn't the bubbly, extravagant guy I knew and liked. I sent him an email, and we agreed to go for a coffee. We both apologised to each other. He told me the medication that he was on made him tired and lose weight easier. He started to cry. He said he felt so lonely and nothing to live for. I put my hand on his hand and reassured him things that things would be ok. I don't know what came over him, but bizarrely, I told him that he could be one of the godparents for my child with Michelle. He smiled profoundly. I reached over and gave him a hug. He looked like he needed it and more throughout the remainder of his life. I felt that making him a godparent would give him the zest to continue the will to live. It was nice to have my 'friend' back in my life.

I had made a bigger effort with Michelle. She was looking bigger. The cravings had started. She liked Sam's chicken fillet burgers. She could get through 3-4 a time. We spoke more. We joked more. There was more affection as well. We were each other's engine, helping to support each other. I felt the love again. It was nice to cuddle up with her in bed even if her belly was massive. I was with a woman that I loved and that all that mattered. It didn't matter that I had another woman pregnant; I could deal with that later. Naturally, as one relationship got better, another relationship deteriorated. As I spent more time with Michelle, I spent less time with Gemma.

Gemma's stomach had got bigger as well. I still continued to fuck her but less than normal. When she showed me baby things she had acquired, I didn't really show much interest. Gemma was just a 'link' that I like fucking and unfortunately got pregnant. It was harsh to view her like that, but that was the harsh reality of it all. Fucking a white girl was one thing, but having and maintaining a relationship was another concept altogether. For me it was a headfuck, and it was an even bigger headfuck as I had impregnated her. Gemma would always say that I had changed and I would always retort that I hadn't. However, I knew I had, and it was because I was in something that I didn't want to be in anymore. "You never stay at mines anymore!" Gemma said to me one day. She looked visibly upset at this. Michelle was getting closer to having the baby, and it was imperative that I was near her at all times and not in the bed of my 'link'. To make it up to her, I told Gemma that I would take her Tinseltown. It was a mistake that I would never forget.

It was a Thursday night. I met Gemma after work. We got to TInseltown and had a real laugh. The food was great, but the desert was even better. I was starting to enjoy her company non sexually again. I noticed it had started to rain.
"Shall we make a move?"
"Yeah, I want one of your cuddles",
I paid the bill and we left. I put Gemma's umbrella over us, as it rained heavily. The weather was wreaking havoc. Thunder and lightning merged from the dark skies. As we started walking, I heard someone shout my name. "Michael, Michael!" Instinctively Gemma and I both turned around. To my surprise and slight aghast, it was Nathan. He looked merry and jovial from the distant, but as he approached us, his countenance turned to utter dismay and disbelief. He was angry and agitated. "What you doing with her?!" he shouted. His question caught me off guard. Was he going to 'bait' me

up? As I was about to respond, Gemma responded with "He is more of a man than you will ever be Nathan!" What was going on?! Did the two of them know each other? "How do you know Nathan?" I asked nervously. Gemma was now the one showing total disdain. "This is the fucking prick that I was seeing, but then he fucked things up, when I caught him getting fucked by a man!" Gemma shouted form the top of her voice. Nathan didn't say anything. Neither did I. Then it clicked. Nathan was Nate that Gemma used to date. How fucked up was this?! What an eerie coincidence this was?! Wanting to avoid further confrontation, I pulled Gemma away from Nathan. However Nathan wasn't having none of it, and stood in our way.

"If he's all man, why has he been fucking me, you and some next bitch who is pregnant with his child?!"

The venom in Nathan's tone was present for all to see. I had been exposed and not on my terms. Exposure never occurs on the terms of a guilty person. "Is it true, is it true?" Gemma protested. I couldn't believe that I had been exposed like that. I couldn't say anything. I was numb with shock. I was also reeling as well. My silence confirmed my guilt.

"CLAP!"

Gemma slapped me in my face. She was snarling like a dog with rabies. "Don't fucking ever come near me again! You make me sick!" Gemma barked, as she tried to run away from myself and Nathan. Nathan then taunted Gemma.

"My dick was better than your weak ass pussy!"

Nathan was all smug. This seemed to ignite a rage within Gemma. She turned direction, barged past me and went for Nathan. The two started scuffling in the street. As I got up to try break them up, Nathan hit a decisive blow. He punched Gemma in her stomach. Gemma seemed to fall to the ground in slow motion, clutching her bulbous belly. Realising what he had done, Nathan ran off. Fucking coward. That would be the last time I would see him. I ran over to Gemma who was clearly in pain. I looked at pregnant belly. I saw blood trickling down her legs. The damage had already been done.

Chapter 25 Gemma

As I lay in the hospital bed, I pondered how my world had shattered the way it did. 24 hours ago, I was a happily pregnant woman enjoying dinner with my 'boyfriend'. Now I'm in hospital bed, devastated, having miscarriage, and to top it off my 'boyfriend' had been fucking my ex boyfriend. How I got deceived like that, I will never know. I never saw that coming, not in a million years. I feel so used, dejected and lonely. This baby was going to my world, our world. I don't know who I hate more, Nathan or Michael, the two 'poofs' I should call them. I touch my belly and it has gone down dramatically. A life that was going to be, gone just like that. God must really not like me. Am I such a bad person? Did I deserve all of this punishment?

I'm angry for various reasons. I hate Nathan because he fucked me over twice, and he killed my baby. I can't believe the faggot punched me in my belly. What a pussy?! He killed my baby. He robbed me of motherhood. May be he did me a favour? Maybe it's a good thing that I'm not having a baby with that shirt lifting Nigger! Can't believe Michael was fucking me and Nathan. The thought makes me feel sick. I don't believe Michael had another girl pregnant. I was incredulously sceptical about this. However, it could be true as Michael never stayed at mine. I can't believe I gave Michael a chance. I said he wasn't a typical 'coon', but he was all along. That 'faggot nigger' got me pregnant. My baby might as well been gay for all it mattered.

Earlier on in the day, my dad told me that Michael had been trying to see me.
"I hope you told him to go to Hell!"
My dad nodded at me. I should have listened to Dad. He was right all along. He told me not to trust them as they would

fuck me over, and that 'coon' did. I started to cry. Dad came over and hugged me. He was gentle with me, as he knew I was still fragile.

"I should have listened to you",

."SHHH",

Dad understood how I was feeling. He could see the remorse and regret in my face and body language towards him. I blamed myself so much. Why I went for that prick I will never know. He questioned my ability to be a woman, and I should have fucked up that faggot for it. What 'man' punches a pregnant woman in the belly? A fucking lunatic! Pride was what got those dumb 'coons' killed when they shoot each other. Pride was the reason I lost my baby. Nathan and Michael are scum. Fucking 'dirty niggers, coons, darkies, black bastards'! Just like the Jews said, 'Never again', never again would I go with a 'nigger'. At that point the nurse came in with my medication. Dad told me he would come and see me later. He was going to leave me by myself, all alone and confused. I swallowed the pills with the water that was given to me. I closed my eyes and tried to sleep, only to think about what could have been... I wanted my Mum!

Chapter 26 Michael

I can't believe what has happened. How could things get so fucked up? How can my life coming crashing back down to Earth again? I must be cursed. I took a deep pull on the zoot. I held it in for about a minute as I try to digest what has happened. I released the weed smoke from my lungs. Just like the smoke, my life looks cloudy, hazy and foggy. I just never saw that coming, Gemma and Nathan, ex partners, yet the way she described him was him all over. I can't believe he punched in her belly, knowing she was pregnant. That something a psychotic bitch would do. Mind you he is a fucking faggot, and the feminine traits are strong in them. I took another pull on the spliff. As I took a pull on the spliff, I contemplated that maybe the crazed faggot did me a favour? That's such a wrong thing to say. It would have been fucked up it if it came out that I had two baby mothers with both, the babies in similar age range. What's fucked up is that Gemma lost the baby, I mean our baby.

I bill up another zoot again, contemplating how things have 'shegged' so badly. I am one baby less, my link doesn't want to know me anymore and that crazed faggot I fucked killed the baby. I took a pull on the zoot. I just want to get high and fly way from this madness. My life was chaotic, and anarchy had descended into it. Could I be Superman and try save it? No I couldn't. I had to accept that I was Batman, the dark knight who tried to get inner peace, but it wasn't happening. I tried to see Gemma, at the hospital, but her old man wasn't having it.

"I have come to see Gemma",

He looked at me with a screwed up face. He was pissed and rightly so. His grandchild was dead. "She doesn't want to see you nigger!" he said harshly. Did he know everything that had happened? Maybe he did. Maybe he didn't. Whatever the situation, he blamed me for the baby's demise. I tried to go past him, but he simply blocked me. "I want to see Gemma, I protested. He grabbed my arm, and looked me dead in the eye. His countenance was heated. Before I knew it he had 'drapsed' me up.

"I told you already nigger, she don't want to see you. If you ever come near her, I'll fucking kill you! You got it?"

He was very adamant by this. I took a gulp before I replied. I didn't want to carry on this confrontation further, so I nodded him in order to appease him, just like Chamberlain had done to Hitler during the Second World War. Gemma's father released his grip, and walked away. White men never attacked on their lone some. They were like wolves; they attacked in packs like what was reflected in the film Football Factory. Hooliganism was glorified yob culture.

All alone in the corridor on this hospital ward, I pondered if I would ever see Gemma again. The answer to this question was no. I tried to call her again after her ordeal, but she never called me back. It was probably the best thing she could do. I fucked up her life once, there was no way she would let me do it twice. I slept with her biggest enemy and was partly responsible for the death of her child. The child's blood was on my hands and there was nothing I could do about it.

I was on my second or third spliff of the day. I was smoking like there was no tomorrow. Smoking weed was a sedentary occupation. Weed was really cathartic for me. It was an outlet for me to let it all out and get problems out of my system. I wanted to kill Nathan. Give me a knife and I would have 'shanked' him. Give me a gun, and I would have shot him. These morbid thoughts were running through my head. Was it because I was smoking skunk? Probably. Was it because I was highly angry and upset? Probably. I wondered how someone who had given me so much pleasure had now given me so much pain. Upon doing the 'deed', Nathan had run off. I had gone to his flat to confront him. I called his mobile a dozen times, but it kept going to his voicemail. I wished that his HIV would turn into AIDS immediately and kill him straight away. He fucked up everything for me. I didn't dislike him. I hated him. He fucked up everything for me. I knocked aggressively at his door, even kicking it, do that he could answer it, and I would knock his fucking block off. I was raging with anger. I could have kicked the door off its hinges, if one of his neighbours hadn't come outside. Nathan was clearly not there or he was hiding just like his sexuality that he once hid in the closet. What was clearly evident now was that his sexuality had come out of the closet and it was wreaking havoc in the process. My spliff was finished. I was high. I was lean. I sat in silence, pondering if I could ever make things right…

Chapter 27 Nathan

This is to whoever wishes to view this letter. Now has come the time that I must go. God has called me to help in his battle against evil. He has spoken to me and I must go immediately. He doesn't care that I am a killer. He doesn't care that I am gay. He only cares that I serve his kingdom and view him as my righteous saviour. I have apologised for all my sins, and the father has blessed me and accepted my apology. This is not hard for me to do. Recent events have showed to me that I am needed else where and now is the time to go. If you read this, tell my mum that I am sorry for being gay and that I love her. Tell Gemma, I'm sorry that I killed her unborn baby. Tell her I am sorry that I messed up her life twice. Tell her I will make it up to her when we meet again in Heaven. I must go now.

God Bless

Chapter 28 Michael

It had been a week since Nathan had been seen at work. No one had heard or seen him. People at work had asked me about his whereabouts, but I was just as clueless as them. It made me wonder did they know about me and him or was I just being paranoid? I still hated him, but my anger had died down now. In amongst the chaos, Michelle was due anytime soon, and that was my priority not that 'faggot'. Nevertheless, I still went and passed by his house to see if the motherfucker was alive.

I got to his house around 7pm. I walked up to his flat to find it boarded up. Had he fucked off to somewhere else? That would be good. He could ruin someone else's life preferably not mine. Just then his neighbour who had seen me attacking his door appeared.

"Have you seen the guy that lived here?"

"Yes I have, and he is dead",

Nathan's neighbour replied so calmly. I looked at him all perplexed and shocked. The neighbour was very stoical about it all. The neighbour continued.

"Poor sod, killed himself. Slit his wrists and overdosed on pills. Saw the paramedics carry out his body"

My shock had now turned to guilt. I felt like a contrite sinner. Did I drive this guy to kill himself?

"When did this happen?"

"Tuesday, his mum found him. Also found a suicide note about him turning religious and apologising for being gay and a killer"

. "SHIT",

"I must run, cheerio"

Our exchange was over just like that. Nathan's life was over just like that. Nathan's neighbour was off like a hawk. I walked away from the flat in shock. I was in a dumbfounded daze.

This guy I knew in more ways than one was dead. I felt for his Mum finding him in that state. How awful. Nathan was no saint, but he didn't deserve to go out like that. Maybe he did. He did kill an unborn baby, but I was no judge. The only person who could judge me was the almighty father whether that is God, ALLAH or whoever people saw as their god. I walked a bit further and sat on a bench. I lit a cigarette pondering all the madness going on around me. At that precise moment, I got a text. I looked at my phone. It was Michelle's mum. Michelle's water had broken, and I was on the go yet again.

Chapter 29 Michelle

"Where the fuck is he?!"

I screamed at my mum, as the contractions got worse. Michael was man enough to fuck me and get me pregnant, but not man enough to help me actually deliver his baby. "He's coming", my mum reassured me. My contractions had started over 3 hours ago. They felt like a long period with constant pains shooting up in belly. The pain was awful. It was hard to explain. I just wanted the baby to come. As I took my surroundings in, everything felt chaotic. The constant flurry and the rushing of doctors and nurses just seem to agitate me. I just wanted Michael here with me and I wanted to have this dam baby. My mum kept on fanning me and wiping sweat from my brow, as the hospital staff checked my vitals. At that point, Michael arrived on the scene. I was so happy to see him. I knew he would keep me sane during this hectic time. He held my hand and kissed my forehead. I felt safe with him by my side. My hysteria and irritation was brought on by the fact that I was scared that myself or my child might not survive. My mum told me that childbirth was the closest I would come to death. At the time, I laughed it off, but now I could see where she was coming from now. I looked around and saw Michael talking to the nurse. He came over back to me. How fitting that as the pain increased, I would bite his head off.

"How you hanging there soldier?"

"How the hell do you think I would feel with all the medics seeing me like this?!"

I screamed from the top of my voice so that everyone could hear how I was feeling. . Michael recoiled like a little child who had been scolded by their parents. I was obviously fit to be telling off my daughter or son when they were born.

Minutes passed, hours dawned and my baby was still not born. Michael and my mum were still around. At this point, I just wanted to have the baby there and there. I was fed up of the nurses and doctors ferrying around me and seeing me in my full morning glory. I was fed up of my mum and Michael constantly checking on me yet I felt lonely, needy and vulnerable. My emotions were all over the place. Tears started to run down my cheek, and usual Michael was there to pick up the pieces. He wiped the tears from my cheek and kissed my forehead.

"Don't worry everything will be ok. I am right here"

This was the reassurance that I needed, the reassurance that I lacked. Michael was definitely my support unit. The nurses and the doctors came back into the room, and asked to speak to Michael. I got scared. Was everything ok? Was the baby ok? I started to panic. I started to fret. My mum held my hand as Michael went and spoke to the medical team. After a few minutes of consultation, Michael came back to Mum and me. Was he going to drop a bombshell? Was he going to crush my heart? I prepared myself for the worst, as Michael approached me. However he smiled at me. I relaxed a little, but I still was anxious to hear what he had to say. "It's ok, the doctors just want to induce you", he said confidently. I had a huge sigh of relief. I watched as the doctor inserted his fingers into me. I like to be fingered when intimate with Michael, but not like this. "You should start to feel some discomfort in a few minutes", the doctor said. I nodded unaware of what was to come. It reminded me of when I popped a Viagra pill with Michael for fun. Just like being induced, nothing happened immediately, but when it did, it really did happen. Out of nowhere, I felt this discomfort that the doctor had informed of, and then an excruciating burning sensation started. I was ready to give birth to this baby. My belly felt like it was on fire. It felt like someone had stuck a hot poker stick in me, and I had to start to get it out of me. The pain was awful. I screamed out in pain. My mum and Michael looked concerned. I needed something for the pain, so one of the nurses gave me an oxygen mask, whilst telling me that I better start pushing for my own good. This gave me the impetus to start pushing like the good little girl that I was. Michael was still by my side now, as I started to push and breathe at the same time. As I kept pushing, the burning pain in my stomach got worse, as the doctors stood guard watching my vagina expand. The pain got so bad that the doctors had to give me an epidural. It didn't do the trick, but it made the pain bearable. I don't really remember the next half an hour, but after many attempts of pushing, I heard the wailing and crying of a little girl. I vaguely remember the cutting of the umbilical cord, but remembered the tears of joy on Michael's face and the ecstasy on my mother's face. The nurses cleaned her, and then put her into my arms and placed into my chest. I looked into her eyes and she looked back at me. Michael was right by my side. We shared a tender kiss. "Well done baby", Michael said as he congratulated me on the birth of our daughter.

"What shall we call her?"

"Let's call her Michaela"

Michael looked like all his Christmas' had come all at once. He was very happy, with that choice of name. He kissed me again. He then went and hugged my mum and the nurses, as he left me for my first moment with Michaela. Again, I looked into her eyes and she looked back at me. She was here. She was beautiful. She was my baby. She was 'our' baby. As I held her, I fell asleep due to the exhaustion in bringing Michaela into the world.

I woke to find myself in another ward. I looked around to see Michael holding Michaela. He looked so good holding her. It looked so right He definitely had the makings to be a good father. As I lay in the bed in pain, it reminded me of a pressing issue that had haunted me throughout the pregnancy and now that Michaela was born. As Michael continued to hold her, a tear rolled down my cheek. I was happy that I had given birth to a healthy beautiful girl. However, there was confusion in my mind, as I pondered how I could ever tell Michael that Michaela might not be his, but might be Ola's?

Chapter 30 Michael

It had been 24 hours since Michaela had been born. She weighed 6lbs and 4 ounces. She was beautiful. She had a full head of hair, my top half and Michelle's bottom half. I was a fervent admirer of my new born daughter. Michelle was resting. She was cream crackered from the previous day's event. Michelle was a tough cookie, a hard one to crack at that. The birth of our daughter marked a new chapter in all of our lives. As I held Michaela, I felt the responsibility of being a father resting on my shoulders. I still couldn't believe that I was a father. I couldn't believe that there was mini me in the world. To think I was nearly a father of two showed me a lot of things about myself. I knew certain things couldn't run no more. The blazing would have to stop immediately. Weed fumes in the home a newborn was not the shout. I might have the odd cigarette, but that would have to be outside. I couldn't be fucking other chicks or other men for that matter. Michaela's birth reaffirmed to me my sexuality and my need to maintain a monogamous relationship. I couldn't be putting my girlfriend and child at risk of sexual diseases or mentally unbalanced people like the deceased Nathan. I was a father now, and I would have to start acting like one. Certain tasks looked unappealing, but I was looking forward to changing nappies and feeding baby. Michaela was my world now. The days of flirting and gallivanting for 'gash' were over. I would need to stay at home and let my bond with my daughter nurture and deepen. I also knew it was quite fitting that the Lord would bless me with a little girl. As a 'gyalist', it was only fitting that I would bear a girl to remind me of my wrong illicit ways. I didn't want to be a typical worthless Black father. I didn't want to be a part time daddy who only saw their child at the weekends or a few months at a time. I wanted to be a full time father and a full time husband as well. Proposing to Michelle would be the next obvious move in this played out saga. It made sense. We lived together, and now we had a daughter together. It seemed natural for us to spend the rest of our lives together. I hoped Michaela's existence would strengthen the loose bonds that we had. Michelle being in labour and giving birth made me realise how much I truly loved her. She was the one that kept me on top. I wanted her more than ever in my life. I knew I had fucked up during the course of the pregnancy by having flings with Gemma and Nathan, but now it felt like God was giving me a second chance to make a 'menz' and redeem myself. I was more than ready to start a fresh. I was ready to run with the ball with both hands all the way to the finishing line. As I got excited at these prospects, Michaela started to cry. I walked around with her to prevent her waking up Michelle. As I held her, I realised that I would need to protect Michaela from all the perils that came with life. I would have to protect her from bad company, danger, illnesses and 'hungry niggas' like me. I would have to protect her from 'hungry niggas' that would promise her the world so that they could have their wicked way with her. I would have to protect her from 'hungry niggas' that would have a large amount of women including my princess on the go, putting them at risk, all for some pussy and a crude ego boost. It was at that point that I realised that I could no longer have my cake and eat it...

THE END

Made in the USA
Lexington, KY
22 April 2012